She pulled the arrow tighter, her heartbeat rising. She need only let go.

Suddenly the bow was snatched from her hand from behind. The arrow once aimed straight and true at her adversary's heart fell harmlessly to the ground. Before she could react, she felt a hand grab her arm.

"In the northern part of the kingdom, that would be murder boy," a distinctly male voice announced.

Held nearly immobile by a powerful grip, Cynthia watched powerlessly as Lord Simon mounted the horse that had been brought to him, heel it into motion and gallop away.

Angrily, she spun as much as the grasp allowed, confronting the man who had hindered her. "I had him in my sights! How dare you interfere with—" Her words died as she locked gazes with the most incredible pair of brown eyes she'd ever seen. She stared, spellbound and open mouthed at their owner.

Hair, the color of a field of wheat, fell to his shoulders. His mouth was outlined with short, carefully groomed facial hair that drew her attention to his full lips. Broad shoulders sat atop what appeared to be a brawny chest, the impression aided by the strength of his grip. She felt the muscles in his arm encircling her waist flex and then release, the pleasant sensation sending warmth through her.

Never before had she allowed a man, especially such a handsome one, to be so close.

Kudos for Kathye Quick

Winner of the Review's Choice Award, Firebrand (Fantasy Romance)

Affaire de Coeur Reviewer's Choice, 5 Stars
--a riveting, complex work of good versus evil worthy of the Hobbit Series and Harry Potter

'Tis the Season (Contemporary Romance) - 2007 Holt Medallion Finalist

Cynthia and Constantine

by

Kathye Quick

This is a work of fiction. Names, characters, places, and incidents either are the product of the author's imagination or are used fictitiously, and any resemblance to actual persons living or dead, business establishments, events, or locales, is entirely coincidental.

Cynthia and Constantine

Contact Information: info@thewildrosepress.com

Cover Art by *Nicola Martinez*

The Wild Rose Press
PO Box 708
Adams Basin, NY 14410-0706
Visit us at www.thewildrosepress.com

Publishing History
First English Tea Rose Edition, 2008
Print ISBN 1-60154-398-0

Published in the United States of America

Dedication

For Mom
To *Cynthia, Jane, Janet, Kelly, Barbara and Joan*
the ladies without whom I could never have brought
this project from idea to book.

Prologue

Sir Constantine of the Court of Camelot brought his sword down in a wide arc, knocking the blade from the hand of the warrior coming over the merlon.

"Fall back," he shouted to his comrades fighting beside him. With a quick snap of the hilt of his sword, he caught the attacker's temple and heaved the slumping figure back over the wall. "Fall back," he called out again. "Or we'll be trapped here. We need to get to the safety of the inner chamber."

As in echo to his words, a thunderous crash shook the fortress as the main gates cracked. Constantine could hear the Saxon horde raise a howl in triumph. With a final groan, the gates collapsed and were heaved aside by the rush of warrior barbarians.

Constantine ran to the edge of the parapet walk and looked down into the courtyard below. The ground appeared crimson as defenders fell beneath the savage assault of swords, stones and bare hands. He tore his gaze away and moved single file along the walkway with his retreating men. As they climbed the stairs to the north tower, the Saxons poured over the walls behind them.

Once through the door, a brother knight, blood streaming from a gash on his forehead, helped Constantine bar the entrance. Others piled chairs and anything movable in front of it.

"Where did they all come from?" the knight shouted, his voice evidence of the panic in his heart. "The Saxons do not usually fight in such numbers this far south of Hadrian's Wall."

Constantine pushed the knight ahead of him, down the stone corridor and into the great hall. "They do today, Sir William. But they go no farther," he vowed. "We make our stand here." He ran a bloodied hand across his brow. Blood spotted his silver mail; some the enemy's, some his comrades, some his own. As he watched the men position themselves for the battle, he wondered what unknown force had united the barbarian tribes so that they fought so fiercely. "Let us hope the riders got through to Camelot," he said grimly.

William put a hand on Constantine's shoulder. "I fear I will never see my home again. Last night I had a vision of my death."

Constantine shrugged it away. "Visions are not truths."

William shook his head. "A truth for sure. If I should meet my end at the point of an enemy sword and should you survive this madness, swear to me that you will deliver a final message to my betrothed."

"Do not worry, William, you will see the face of your intended again."

William's face hardened. "By a knight's honor, before this battle begins, swear to me," he repeated, reaching out his hand.

Constantine hesitated for a moment and then nodded, clasping William's forearm sealing the vow. The depth of William's conviction shone in his eyes. "We'll go to her together," Constantine assured.

“Nay, I feel this day is my last,” William said, as a great rumble rose from behind the outer door. He clamped his hand on Constantine’s arm. “Hear me. Before I left nearly ten years ago to join the Crusades, John Locke granted me the hand of his daughter, Cynthia. She was a mere child of twelve years. Locke desired to take up the quest also, but it would leave Cynthia alone. His wife had since passed. I bade them take up residence in Leyborne Castle for their protection. She would be cared for by a nursemaid and tended to by the nursemaid’s daughter. When Cynthia became of marriageable age and upon my return, I would take her as my wife.”

“And return you will,” Constantine assured.

“Please, there is no time to debate the issue.”

Seeing both the fear and the petition in William’s eyes, Constantine fell quiet.

“First Cynthia’s father falls in battle, a great sorrow for her indeed. Now, as we return from the Quest and are about to part ways for our homes, we come upon this Saxon horde raiding the villages and taking all they can. The code of chivalry must be honored, and I do not fear the fight, but the Almighty whispered my fate in my ear and I must heed his words. So I ask you now, if I fall in this battle and the Almighty’s Grace smiles upon you, will you travel to Leyborne Castle and deliver my final will?”

Eyes locked with that of his brother knight, Constantine nodded. “By a knight’s honor, I vow it.”

“Tell Cynthia that all my lands and worldly possessions now belong to her as if we had been bound in marriage. Tell her to find a champion, marry well, and be happy." He pulled the bloodied glove from his left hand. "Take this ring emblazoned with my family crest from my lifeless hand and deliver it to her. Then take Cynthia and the ring to the Bishop and record this verbal will and testament. It will protect her so none but her may lay claim to my lands and all that I own, and try to take the bequest I give you now from her."

A sudden resounding crash cut any further words as the Saxons battered against the doors of the great hall. Constantine nodded his agreement to William and they moved away from the crude barrier and into the center of the room. There they watched the boards begin to split around the edges of the door and heard the sound of pounding fill the air much like the toll of the funeral knell. Poised for battle, teeth gritted with resolve, they waited for the inevitable.

"You've done the King proud today," Constantine shouted above the awful sound of wood splintering. Gripping his shield tighter so it would not slip from his hand he braced himself for the onslaught. "Let us give the Saxons a reason to remember the Knights of Camelot."

Chapter One

"My lady! He comes."

Ignoring the anxious shout of her handmaiden, Jane, Cynthia Locke of Abertaine stared out at the distant hills from the balcony of her chamber. The morning breeze caught her hair, sending the golden strands dancing around her face. She brushed them back with her hand and tucked the tendrils behind her ears even as her blue eyes continued to scan the horizon. The morning sun had not yet burned off the mist that clung to the low lying fields, making the area surrounding the castle look draped in magic. In the foreground, a rider emerged, cutting through the haze on his way to the village.

If only that rider would be Sir William retuning, Cynthia thought. Then the madness would stop and calm would return to the shire. But it had been nearly five years since William returned to the castle, and then only for a day when he brought her father's body home to the pyre. Five years earlier her father and William pledged their swords to Arthur joining his quest for a united England.

"Cynthia! Please!" Jane called, the tone of her voice more anxious, "Come in from the balcony. He..."

The sound of a light scuffle roused Cynthia from her reverie. Even before she turned, she knew who would be there.

"If you wish to jump, I'd suggest the North Tower. It's higher."

Any time she heard it, the sound of Lord Simon's voice grated on her, but today its quality sounded particularly revolting. "I would not give you the pleasure," Cynthia countered, turning slowly to face him "or the satisfaction of a legal claim to this manor. William will be here soon enough to claim both his bride-to-be and his home."

"A man who leaves his property unprotected just to ride off to take up the foolish charge of an irrational king is either mad or has been bewitched by a heathen Druid," Simon scoffed.

"Neither," Cynthia said, quickly rising to William's defense. "By his honor William and my father set off to join Arthur and his Knights in their noble cause."

Simon laughed. "Arthur's noble cause is nearly at an end. Even as we speak Mordred gains allies."

"You among them."

"Indeed." He loosened the clasp of the cloak across his shoulders and let it fall to the floor in a dark purple puddle. Turning slightly, he kicked it carelessly in Jane's direction. When Jane hesitated in gathering it up, Simon took a step toward her and raised a gloved hand, angling it to her face.

Cynthia quickly stepped forward. "Lay a hand on her and I swear you'll wish you'd not awoken this morning." Disgust deepened her voice.

Simon looked from Jane's face to Cynthia's and slowly lowered his hand. His gaze then raked first across Cynthia's body and then Jane's. "Best you remember that I tolerate the vassal only because I desire her lady."

"You desire what will never be. I have pledged my love to another," Cynthia said quickly.

Simon laughed, the callousness of his tone echoing in the still morning air. "I care not for your love, Lady Cynthia." His gaze fell to the rise and fall of her breasts. "It is your body that incites my blood."

"My body is bound to my love, and only to he who will be my husband will I offer it."

Simon took a step toward her. She did not step back, but held his gaze, daring him to make his move.

"Be grateful you still hold sway over the people of the shire," Simon said, balling his hands into a fist, an obvious attempt to channel his anger. "For now." His gaze moved from Cynthia to Jane. "But one day soon you and your vassal will wish you both could watch the sun rise from my bedchamber."

Cynthia ignored the innuendo of his words and walked to the fallen cloak. She snatched it from the floor and held it out to Jane. "Take this down to the kitchen and have one of the maids brush it clean. We wouldn't want Lord Simon to tarry longer than necessary."

Reluctantly Jane took it from her. "I don't wish to leave you alone with him."

"Lord Simon will be leaving anon," Cynthia replied.

Jane nodded and quickly left the room.

Simon waited until the heavy chamber doors closed before speaking. "So, I see a fire burns in the lady." Slowly he removed his leather gloves and circled Cynthia as he slapped them repeatedly into the palm of his left hand. "I am very good at taming wild stallions. Passionate women are no different, I'm told. One day I will have the benefit of your fire."

Cynthia lifted her chin. "Then I would indeed make use of the North Tower."

"As you wish," he said, no vestige of caring in his voice.

As he moved around her, Cynthia watched him carefully. A tall man, well proportioned and solidly built, with his dark curls and equally dark eyes, many ladies undoubtedly even considered him handsome. But she knew his heart and no measure of comeliness could disguise what lay there.

"A woman of substance would serve me well," Simon continued. "Are you ready to acknowledge that William is dead and you have no protector?"

"Nay," she said firmly, trying to step around him even as he positioned his body to prevent it. "William will return home and I will honor the covenant made by my father." The conviction in her words hid the doubt in her heart.

She was a child when her father betrothed her to William. For the short time before he and her father left, William had treated her well, more like a sister than a wife-to-be. But he still made it clear to all that when he returned from the quest, she would be the lady of the household. From that day, no man in court dared treat her with the insolence Simon made known today, or dared to look upon her the way he had. No longer a child, she clearly recognized the desire she saw in his eyes.

How long could she hold off Simon's advances, she did not know. When William returned to Camelot after paying tribute to her father, she hoped he would return again quickly. But long days stretched into lonely nights with all dispatches from him stopping nearly a fortnight ago. Although a sense of foreboding built around her like one of the thick castle towers, that was something Simon would ever see.

“Come now, Cynthia,” Simon said, stepping closer to her, “Do you tell me that you do not get lonely waiting for a ghost?” He reached out and touched her face with the back of his hand, a gesture so intimate in nature that it made Cynthia step backward.

“For William only,” she assured.

Simon’s hand shook as he lowered it. “The money left for your care runs low and, being unwed, you have no claim to any assets here. It would be wise for you to take a husband.”

Cynthia did not know what angered her more; the reminder that she was nearly penniless or the choice he seemed to be offering her. Both equally disturbed her.

“I can make my own way,” she said icily. “I need no help from the likes of you.” She saw anger explode on Simon’s face the minute her words were out.

“My patience wears thin,” he said, grasping her shoulder and digging his fingers into the soft flesh he found there. “Soon you will have no choice.”

Cynthia clenched her teeth in anticipation of the pain as she jerked her body backward. As she did, the shoulder of her gown gave way, allowing her to escape his grasp. She rushed out of the room and down the stone stairs to the safety of the rapidly filling courtyard.

****

Simon watched Cynthia leave, anger and arousal warring inside him. As always she managed to heat his temperament as well as his body.

Soon he would bring her to task on both.

****

Just as Jane put her hand on the door of the castle keep Simon grabbed her arm from behind. His purple cape fell from her hand as she struggled to free herself. "Let me go," she said from between clenched teeth, wincing at the way his fingers dug into her flesh.

"Your lady was not very cooperative today, wench. Perhaps you will be more so," he countered, his gaze dropping to her breasts.

Jane tugged against his grip. "I would rather die."

"That could be arranged," he said, his mouth a sneer.

Before she could react, he caught her free hand with his and jerked her forward. Soon his arms encircled her waist, his hands locking hers behind her back.

"They say Druid women know how to evoke a man's darkest desires through their potions and powders" Simon continued, his lips grazing Jane's cheek as he spoke.

"My Lord," Jane said from between clenched teeth, "the old ways are dying, especially since you have sent all those you found who still practice the arts to Mordred for his use against Arthur."

"Perhaps not all. I have heard there may be one or two left. You among them." He hugged her closer. "I have never bedded a Druidess," he whispered into her ear.

"And you never will," Jane returned, anger coloring her voice as she struggled against his hold.

"Ah yes," Simon said, his voice more like a growl, its tone husky, making clear his rising excitement as Jane's efforts to free herself only drove her deeper into his body. "You feel good against me." His knee split her legs. His thigh rubbed against her mound with his carnal movements.

He leaned forward intent on closing the distance between their mouths when the distinctive hiss of an arrow slicing the air passed his ear. It hit the stone wall next to his head with a ping before falling to the ground.

With a curse, he released Jane and stumbled backward. He steadied himself and turned to find the archer. Ten paces behind him stood Cynthia with another arrow readily aimed in his direction.

"My Lord, I pray the arrow did not graze you," Cynthia said in a firm voice, her gaze lined perfectly down the shaft of the arrow. "I fear my aim is a bit off today." She shifted the bow to the right and then quickly returned it to aim.

Simon looked to where she had gestured. A target-draped mound of hay with four arrows dead center sat in front of the far stone wall. His eyes flared. "Much to my good fortune."

Cynthia pulled the arrow tighter. Light spangled along the taut bowstring like the rays around the edge of the sun. She dropped her gaze to the garment at his feet. "My Lord, I see that your cloak is ready."

One side of Simon's mouth pulled into a sneer. "One day I will teach both you and your handmaiden your places."

"But today you will retrieve your cloak and leave us," Cynthia said.

"You have little time left to be so bold," he countered. Snatching up his cape, he spun on his heels and stalked off.

Jane let out a breath she did not realize she was holding and walked to Cynthia. "He said he would have me in your place."

Cynthia lowered the bow and allowed the string to slacken. "'Tis folly to think he'd have either of us."

"I thank the Almighty you aim as true as you did when you won the tournament in the village."

Cynthia shook her head. "Nay, I do not. I intended for his head."

****

Constantine rode long into the night to deliver the terrible news and was not eager to find the lady whose heart he would surely break. He cleared the forest surrounding Leyborne Castle and pulled up on the reigns, bringing his horse to a halt. Darkness draped the castle save for some light coming through the arrow-loops on the towers and from guard posts on the wall walk.

Constantine leaned forward and patted the horse on the side of his neck. "Easy boy," he said as the horse took a few steps backward. "I agree. The lady should rest easy tonight. This news will keep. You need rest, and so do I." He pulled back on the reigns and the horse turned. Gently, he heeled the steed in the ribs and headed back into the woods.

An open path led him through the moonlight. It sliced its way uphill through the forest to a crest where he could see the glimmer of the village lights. Then it turned downward again until he rode out of the forest and onto a more level plain in which sat rows of houses and shops.

He slowed the horse to a trot and followed the sound of loud voices and bawdy laughter to a large double building near the village center. Dismounting, he spied a lad of what he guessed about ten years of age, and motioned for him to approach.

"Do you know a place where my horse can rest and be fed?" he asked the boy.

"For a price," the boy replied.

Constantine reached into his saddle pack on his horse and pulled out a black velvet purse. From inside he took a coin and flipped it to the boy.

After catching it with both hands, the lad took the coin between two fingers and held it up. His eyes widened. "'Tis gold." He looked up at Constantine. "Stolen?"

"Nay. Earned. Is it enough?"

The lad nodded. "Aye. Enough to bed the steed for many nights."

"How much then for a man?" He handled the boy the reigns.

The lad tossed his head. "If you have more, there's food and drink inside. And a place to stay if the owner takes a likin' to you."

Constantine patted the horses rear quarter as it passed. "Then I shall make sure of it."

****

Cynthia's mind filled with fright. Each day that passed without word from William, Simon had grown bolder. It would only be a matter of time before he tried to make good on his threat. She vowed that she would be prepared when that happened.

Jane came in with a tray filled with milk, cheese, peaches and grapes. "You haven't eaten all day. You are the lady of the manor and must keep up your strength." She set the tray on a small table.

"You're right," Cynthia said, taking some grapes. "This place is my home insofar as I have one. Remember when I first came? You stood behind your grandmother, watching me. Every time I caught your eye, you'd duck back behind her skirts. It became a game."

Jane smiled. "Each time I peeked around her, you'd be closer. Then all of a sudden, when I peeked past her, you were right there next to me, and we both laughed so hard that we cried."

Cynthia returned the smile. "That day changed my life. With no family, save my father and no real home, William took me in and now I have both."

Jane lowered her eyes. "With Gram gone to her reward and my mother run off, I only have you."

"And a fine pair we are," Cynthia said, laughing. "A commoner posing as a Lady…"

"And a Druid posing as a handmaiden," Jane finished for her.

Cynthia glanced out the window. She could see Simon in the middle bailey with a small contingent of his soldiers. "It was once peaceful here." She looked back at Jane. "And I swear, one day, it will be that way again."

****

The Boar's Head Inn was alive with the anticipation of the May Day celebration. Men and women gathered around crude wooden tables sampling the latest batch of ale. Constantine sat at the back finishing a plate of carrots and fish, watching the interaction of the villagers.

"Another round?"

He looked up. The innkeeper's wife prepared to pour more ale into the wooden cup in his hand. Constantine straightened and declined with a polite shake of his head, the motion freeing the medallion around his neck from his tunic.

The women set her pitcher of ale on the table. "I know these markings," she said fingering the pendant. "You be a knight?"

Constantine took the medallion from her hand and tucked it back inside his tunic. "Perhaps."

"Then you best be keepin' that to yourself. 'Tis dangerous for a knight," she glanced around the inn, "a knight alone here in the shire."

Constantine raised his cup. He knew it would cost him a penny and more ale to continue engaging the woman in conversation to find out more. "Then I hope, good lady, that you also will be keeping my secret safe."

"I make no promises," she replied, filling his cup. "With Lord Simon pledging his sword to Mordred, he don't take kindly to strangers. If he thought I be harborin' one of Arthur's knights...." She stopped and ran her thumb across her neck.

"Lord Simon?"

"Aye. Lord of the manor and all the lands surrounding for a hundred miles."

Constantine raised a dark eyebrow. "I was told these lands belong to Sir William Leyborne. Did I take a wrong turn in coming?"

The innkeeper's wife shook her head, her brown hair dancing around her round face. "Nay. Once was his. No more. Lord Simon come and took it all."

"And the Lady of the manor?"

"Poor child. Lady Cynthia puts up a good front, but she's a prisoner. Nowhere to go and no means to get there if she did have a place. Much like all of us."

"I have a message for her, from William."

The innkeeper's wife shook her head. "If William is not deliverin' it, then I fear he is dead. As you will be also if you try to bring it to her. His Lordship fancies her for his wife. Don't allow her visitors." She looked him up and down. "Especially ones with eyes like heaven and a body fine enough to take a woman there." She started to say more when a loud voice rose from behind her.

"Woman, more ale for the thirsty!" Large hands spun her around. "Unless you be wasting it all on that one."

Constantine rose, noticing the large hands on the waist of the innkeeper's wife matched the size of their owner. His matted mass of hair hung to his shoulders, blending with the beard that framed his face. A stained tunic and brawny arms distinguished him as either a blacksmith or herdsman; a man worth respecting. Constantine did not want to call attention to himself, but chivalry demanded a lady in distress be rescued. The innkeeper's wife struggled but to no avail. Constantine could tell she did not want to be there so chivalry must be served!

"Good sir," Constantine said, I just engaged the lady in conversation. I did not mean to keep her from her work."

The large man laughed. "Lady? Where?"

A few of the patrons also broke into laughter. "Gamel don't know no ladies," one of them called out.

"A lady right here," Constantine replied, bowing and kissing the back of the innkeeper's wife's hand. He lifted his gaze back to the man holding her. "Are you a bargaining man, Gamel?"

"What kind of bargain?"

"Let the lady go, and I'll spot the hard-working men here to a pint of ale."

Gamel didn't hesitate. He spun the innkeeper's wife out of his grasp and gave her a hardy whack on her backside. "Off you go. You heard the man. Ale!" The patrons erupted into cheers as Gamel threw his arms around Constantine. "I think you be gettin' the short end of the bargain."

Constantine grimaced with the pressure of the bear hug. "You'll need both hands for the ale."

Gamel laughed. Soon the cups overflowed with ale and the men folk drank contentedly.

Constantine took a healthy swig of warm ale and contemplated his predicament. In light of what he just learned, it appeared that making a vow in battle would be a lot easier than keeping it. But he knew he could not leave until he completed the charge given him.

A commotion near the door interrupted his thoughts as two soldiers came into view and headed straight for him. "Stranger. State your business," the taller of them demanded.

Constantine drained the last of the ale and set the cup on the table. He slowly lifted his head and locked his gaze with the soldier but said nothing.

The soldier's hand went to the hilt of the dagger on his belt. "I ask you again, state your business."

A group of men crowded around them. Constantine knew he would have no allies among the villagers. His mind spun with a means to calm the growing tension.

"I come from Devonshire," he replied. "Looking for work and a place to stay for a time."

"Then you best be going back. His Lordship hires no vassals for his lands. He prefers to administer to his court and his fief, himself." The soldier's hand gripped the dagger at his belt tighter.

"I asked him here. I be wantin' to liven up the place," the innkeeper's wife suddenly said from across the room. She walked to a vat of ale and picked up a lute lying on the floor next to it. "Here, minstrel," she said tossing Constantine the instrument. "Sing for yer supper."

Constantine caught it, and in a fluid motion raised it to his chest and began to play. Fortunately his mother insisted her children learn the gentler aspects of life along with the skills of knighthood taught by his father. He strummed the beginning to one of her favorite songs grateful he had paid attention to her lessons. Soon the gentle sound of the lute drowned out the loud voices around him.

He began to sing, his voice mellow and soothing. Walking around the inn, he stopped at tables, the song telling a tale of quests, battles and love. It ended amid cheers.

"Another!" a patron soon shouted.

"A love song," said another

"Nay, battle songs," suggested a third.

"Soon enough," the innkeeper's wife replied, bringing Constantine another cup of ale. "For your parched throat, minstrel," she said placing emphasis on the last word.

"I owe you much, good woman," he said.

"Aye, you do." As he began to drink she whispered, "You can have the room at back end beyond the curtains until you do what you come to do. But best you do it quickly and be on your way. Until then, another song as payment for the room."

Constantine began to strum once more; looking around the room, he noticed the soldiers had gone. Thanks to the quick thinking of the inn's matron, his identity appeared safe for now.

Chapter Two

Cynthia felt the blood race though her body. From her hiding place among the rows of trees lining the forest clearing, her blue eyes studied the soldiers packing camp and getting ready to move on. They would not see her. She wore a peasant's tunic that came to her knees, green to blend into the bushes and trees shielding her. Her legs were covered by dark brown leggings the color of rich bark to further hide her from sight. She'd tied the large shirt around her waist with a length of cord. A brown cowl covered her blond hair to complete the disguise.

Like a scout sent to evaluate the strength of an enemy before battle, she again scanned the area. The large tent in the center of the clearing had to be Simon's.

She planned this risky act from moment she'd found out that Simon planned on taking out the hawk. She knew what she had to do and prayed for the courage to do to.

She took a deep breath and closed her eyes, summoning all her strength and nerve. When she opened them, he was there, a mere hundred yards separating him from her. She watched him gesture to his soldiers with animated movements, clearly agitated. The soldiers rushed to comply with whatever command he gave them. Within moments, most mounted their horses and sped away, leaving only five behind.

Simon took a step forward and surveyed the area, his gaze halting at the place where she hid. She smothered the gasp that rose in her throat and held her breath. Could he see her? She could hear her heartbeat thundering in her ears as she dared not move for fear of discovery. Endless seconds passed as she stood perfectly still, waiting for either detection or deliverance. After what seemed like a lifetime, he turned and went back inside his tent.

Feeling her body release, she reaffirmed her decision. She raised the bow set firmly in her left hand and reached behind with her right removing an arrow from the quiver slung across her back. With a practiced hand, she set the arrow in place and pulled back on the string. Raising the bow to eye level, she touched the string to her cheek to center her aim and looked down the shaft of the arrow. From her vantage point, nothing stood between her and the entrance to the tent. The metal tip at the end was perfectly aimed at the center opening. Simon need only appear once more.

Her arm quivered slightly as she waited. She knew what she was about to do was risky, but she saw it as the only way she knew to really be free of him.

Then suddenly he appeared just outside the tent flap, Lord Simon of Cowell, taking in what Cynthia hoped would be his last breath of air. She pulled the arrow tighter, her heartbeat rising. She need only let go when suddenly from behind her, a hand snatched the bow from her hand. The arrow once aimed straight and true at her adversary's heart fell harmlessly to the ground. Before she could react, she felt a hand grab onto her arm.

"In the northern part of the kingdom, that would be murder, boy," a distinctly male voice from behind her said.

Held nearly immobile by a powerful grip, Cynthia watched powerlessly as Simon mounted the horse that had been brought to him, heel it into motion and ride away.

Angrily, she spun as much as the grasp allowed, confronting the man who hindered her so blatantly from securing her freedom. "I had him in my sights! How dare you interfere with—" She stopped, her words cut as her gaze locked with the most incredible pair of brown eyes she had ever seen. She stared, spellbound and open mouthed at their owner.

Hair, the color of a field of wheat, fell to his shoulders. Short, carefully groomed facial hair outlined his mouth and drew her attention to his full lips. Broad shoulders sat atop what appeared to be a brawny chest, the impression aided by the strength of his grip. She felt the muscles in the hand on her arm flex and then release, the pleasant sensation sending warmth through her. Never before had she allowed a man, especially such a handsome one, to be so close to her.

"Is that not the law here also?" he asked, tossing her bow into the thicket.

"To kill a thief is justice, not murder," she countered looking back in the direction Simon had taken. She turned back to him. As she jerked her arm in an attempt to free herself, a golden ringlet freed itself from the cowl on her head.

His other hand reached out and brushed the hood back completely exposing her hair. "You're a woman," he remarked.

She tried to pull away again, but he did not allow it. She felt warmth course again through her skin and up her arm. "Justice has no gender," she countered.

"I saw a man with no need to steal. His tent flew the banner of a nobleman, and he had soldiers not bandits to command. But I find a woman in boy's garb ready to take his life."

"You do not know that man and cannot judge him in just one glance." She met his eyes and did not try to step away from him. "Nor can you judge me."

"Then neither can I judge if your charge rings true and allow the arrow to fly."

She held his gaze, the pulse beating rapidly at the base of her throat betraying her anger. "Turn and leave, stranger. I still have time to complete my task."

"My name is Constantine," he said. "Now, no longer a stranger, I wish to know your quarrel with the man." His gaze traveled across her face before it settled on her mouth.

Cynthia felt heat rise on her cheeks as his gaze continued to linger on her mouth. Although close enough for her to see that gold lay among the deep rich brown of his eyes, she still did not step back. With effort she controlled the urge to trace the curve of the high cheekbones that seemed emphasized by his full lips that now curled into a smile.

She lowered her gaze to his mouth and then raised it meaning to give him a stern reply, but when their eyes met, a pull she found hard to resist filled her. She could smell citrus and musk as his scent rose from his body. She breathed in the pleasant aroma and suddenly forgot the words she meant to say. In the span of a heartbeat, the world as she knew it somehow shifted and then realigned with the essence of this man branding itself inside her.

She blinked to fade the feeling from her soul. His presence muddled her senses, but her charge remained clear.

"This is not your concern," she said. "I will finish what I came to do. Be on your way, Constantine," she cautioned with a toss of her head. "Leyborne Shire is no place for strangers."

Suddenly men appeared from either side of the thicket and encircled them.

"It seems your words ring true." Constantine said drawing his sword in response to theirs. He let go of her arm and stepped protectively in front of her. Widening his stance in a defensive posture, he waited for them to make their move. "If you are as handy with that bow as you say you are, perhaps I should not have disarmed you so quickly," he said to her.

Cynthia did not respond.

"Stand down, stranger," one of the men ordered. "There is no escape."

"I intend none," Constantine returned. Confusion darted across his face as one of the men retrieved the bow from the thicket and handed it to the woman he had disarmed. "I planned to champion the lady, but it seems I need not."

"We should take no prisoners if we are to catch Lord Simon," another of the men said, the implication in his voice clear.

Cynthia slipped the bow across her shoulders. She glanced at Constantine, a sly smile spreading across her face as she looked him up and down. "He can go. He's no threat." Hearty laughs rose with her words as the men sheathed their swords. She turned to leave.

Constantine put his hand on her arm to stop her. "Wait."

The men drew their weapons in response.

"I am Constantine, a knight in the court of Arthur of Camelot." He slowly lowered his blade. "By the king's law, I have the right to know your issue here."

Cynthia felt her heartbeat rise. A knight. Alone. Where was William? Her stomach clenched with fear, but she needed to stay strong. "This fight is not yours," she said to him, hoping her voice did not reveal her uncertainties.

"If you are in danger, it is," Constantine disagreed.

"Good knight," she tossed her head in the direction Simon had gone, "the distance between us and the real threat grows longer with each second we waste. The scoundrel has taken what is not his to own. He corrupts the land with his mere presence and oppresses us all. Each day he steals our hopes and our dreams. A disease such as that cannot be cured but must be cut from the body."

Constantine eyes searched Cynthia's face. The tilt of her head, the tone of her body language left no doubt to the sincerity of her claim. He sheathed his weapon and nodded to her. "Then I believe I owe you an apology."

"You owe me your sword in assistance," she countered.

From behind them, a soldier rode in. All turned to him. "Milady, Lord Simon rides to Donahyde Castle to meet with Mordred and his forces." The horseman wheeled his mount in a tight uneasy turn.

Cynthia's shoulders slumped. "Then we have failed. The moment is gone."

Chapter Three

Once again Constantine stopped Cynthia as she turned to leave. "Lady, I cannot let you leave until I know the reason you would risk forfeiting your life to kill a man."

Several of Cynthia's loyalists moved to protect her. She waved away their help. "Go back to the castle," she said to them.

"One of us should stay with you," the one closest to her protested.

"The lady need not fear me," Constantine offered. "I swear by my honor she will be safe enough."

The soldier turned to Cynthia. "But if Lord Simon returns and finds you missing, his anger will fall upon your handmaiden."

"Simon should be the one in fear if that should happen. Besides, Donahyde Castle lies a full day's ride ahead," Cynthia said folding her arms across her chest and staring at the cloudless sky. "I won't tarry long." She walked to a nearby tree and leaned against it, watching as the men mounted their horses and rode off.

She watched Constantine walk to her, hand instinctively on the hilt of his sword in its scabbard at his side. Never had she seen his like. His gray tunic draped over a rock hard body toned by years of training. He strode with shoulders back emphasizing the breadth of them. She felt his gaze on her as he came closer. Hot, powerful, it flared as mesmerizing as it was wary. In it she saw deep intelligence but also a guarded look kept his emotions well hidden telling her nothing.

This man, this handsome man, could equally be a knight sent by Arthur to give her news or a spy sent by Simon to test her. She dared not give him too much information until she determined which.

She sat down on a broad, gnarled stump next to the tree and laid her bow on the ground beside her. "Tell me, why is it that a knight rides so far from Camelot?"

"Why would you ask me that?" His tone mirrored the confusion in his eyes. "Knights are charged with protecting the King and his people. In Arthur's quest for a united England, all citizens are to be safeguarded, no matter how far from Camelot."

"I meant to only make conversation."

"Then tell me more of this Simon," Constantine said, settling in a firm stance in front of her. "What has he done to incur the wrath of a wood nymph?"

His bold assessing stare felt as intimate as a caress to her skin and brought instant heat to her cheeks. She lowered her eyes, remembering her mannish garb. "He rides with the Saxons and makes blood pacts with those who oppose Arthur's rule." She raised her chin and caught his gaze. "Mordred the latest."

She saw concern move across his face, but he quickly reined it. "Why does he roam so free on lands that belong to William of Leyborne?" Constantine asked.

"Because he can," Cynthia quickly returned, hearing the anger bubble in her voice.

"William left no soldiers to protect what he holds dear?"

"He did, but most were killed in the battle with Simon when he first attacked. Those that remained were given the choice to join Simon's army or join their comrades on the pyre."

"And the men with you today? Did they not wear his colors?"

"Strong of purpose we may be, but neither strong of arms nor numbers."

"William would have rewarded their loyalty."

"Would have?" Cynthia felt her heartbeat rise in response to the implication in his words. She stood to meet his eyes.

"Aye. I knew William's heart and his keenness for his land. It is because of him that I am here."

Cynthia swayed slightly and leaned closer to the tree to keep from falling. A buzzing noise filled her ears as her breath quickened. "I fear you made a long journey for naught," she said, feeling dread fill her heart and turn it cold. "He has not yet returned home."

She saw his gaze drift over her shoulder and study the gray bark of the tree on which she rested. When it returned to her face, sadness draped his eyes. "That I know. I come to give his lady a message."

Cynthia's heart leapt to her throat. Her mind whirled with terrible thoughts and she nearly screamed at him not to speak. Inside she somehow knew what would come, but if he did not say the words aloud, then perhaps it would not be. In front of her Constantine's face faded and blurred as if her eyes had filled with tears.

She looked at him in silence for a long moment. When she at last found the strength, the words came out in a rush of air. "I am his lady. I am Cynthia."

She heard the breath flood from his lungs. "Then you must steel yourself, milady, for the news I bring is grave."

She felt a single tear trail down her cheek. "Then tell me quickly then, for if you are to slay me with your words, make it a swift strike rather than a slow, measured thrust."

A sound she suspected was an oath came from him right before the awful words. "William has fallen in battle."

Sorrow poured over her and she began to cry. Not softly, like a proper maiden's grief, but in great sobs that shuddered though her body until the strength in her legs finally gave way and, still sobbing, she fell to ground on her knees.

Constantine knelt and tightened his arms around her shoulders. The force of her weeping shook her whole body and he feared she would lose consciousness from the violence of it. The loss of Sir William clearly stole all measure of her composure.

"Please, my lady, be calm," he murmured against her cheek. "William was a good man, a fine knight. He thought only of you and his home as he faced the prospect of his mortality."

"If Lord Simon discovers William's fate, all is lost," Cynthia replied, her voice shaky.

"Do not despair. Hope did not fade out with his life." Even as he spoke, he looked around the glade. "If what you say is true, we must be wary. If someone hears us, your fate is sealed. The matter of William's bequest still looms uncertain, having not yet been filed and, without his written protection, another claim can be placed before your own. We should not talk here. We need a place, safe, somewhere spies would not listen. Do you know such a place?" he gently asked her.

But even as his arms tensed around her, she did not seem to be able to stop herself from weeping. Tears ran down her cheeks and sobs clogged her throat.

"Come," he said urging her to standing with him. "Come away with me."

Cynthia lifted her head, her eyes red but glistening silver from her tears. "I cannot. I cannot leave the people in his hands."

"Lady, not to flee." He released her from his embrace and took her hands in his. "To talk of William and of his covenant to you even in his final hours."

Cynthia said nothing, but only continued to look into his eyes. The waning day's sun bathed Constantine in its light, painting the colors of sunset into his hair. He looked to her like an angel come to save her. But he was only a man and she feared her plight beyond saving.

Constantine returned her gaze in silence for a long moment before dropping his eyes to her lips. When his gaze returned to her, she could see a struggle inside the warm brown of his eyes. His hand raised and then stopped an inch away from her face and held there, as if he were fighting the temptation to touch her face. Instead, he took her hand, urged her to her feet and led her to his horse.

"There is nothing you can do for him now, Lady Cynthia. But you can protect what he loved most," he advised.

She let him settle her on the horse's back and huddled in the saddle. Constantine trusted his horse to stay steady and retrieved the lady's bow. There should be no evidence that she had been in the woods this day. He gave it to her and she clutched it like a talisman. In one swift motion he mounted behind her and, grasping the reins, encircled her with his arms.

The early spring air hung cool around them and she shivered against his chest. She felt him tense, straightened her back and turned her head. Her eyes, glassy from weeping, seemed to jolt him. He dropped his gaze from their steely blue color to her neck, showing him skin gone too far pale in her grief.

"Lady, again I must ask. Is there a place we can speak in private, away from ears that may waiting for news such as that I have?" he asked her again.

"Not far from here is a monastery," she said softly. "Most of it burned and lay to ruins by Simon and his men, but still home to a shepherd who still tends to his flock. The friar will allow us there.

Constantine nodded and urged the horse to an easy gallop.

****

As Constantine rode with Cynthia cradled between his arms he could not help but wonder about the terrible situation he found. William did not know of the dire situation of his shire or else he would have hurried to defend it. Of that Constantine was sure.

But how could it have happened. Surely William had couriers who brought news of his home to court. Had they all been killed by Simon? Why had William not sent a courier back to Leyborne Castle when all news had stopped?

Constantine would have no answers until Lady Cynthia recovered herself from the terrible shock of William's death.

He grit his teeth. He may not know much at this point, but he would not leave her or the people unprotected. That he did know.

****

Shrouded by shadows cast by the coming night the man watched the rider hoist Cynthia onto his horse and ride away. There was not enough light to give the watcher a view of the man's face, but he could clearly see the shield hanging from the horse's saddlebow.

The crimson lion of Arthur. A knight of Camelot.

Under the man's watchful eye, the knight turned into the forest leaving behind the trails of prints from the horse.

The man in the shadows smiled. At the right time, there was profit to be made here.

Chapter Four

The light from the rising moon barely showed the crumbling monastery ahead. It appeared a harsh place to take a lady. Piles of leaves and fallen branches lay around charred wood and toppled stones, showing it more a refuge for transients or those in flight rather than a house of God. But a newly thatched roof over what appeared could have been the chapel told Constantine there could be some warmth and shelter afforded inside.

He carefully dismounted and held out his hand. "Come, my lady. You can rest a while."

Her hand felt cold as ice when he took it, and he held on tightly so she would feel safe. Knowing his mount would not wander away, he led her through the torn, dirty cloth serving as a door. Inside the dying coals of a fire offered just enough light for him to see the remains of an altar with a chipped cross adorning its center. At first glance, the makeshift chapel appeared empty; the person keeping it in service to the Lord nowhere in sight. Constantine took careful stock of the surroundings. To be certain.

"Rest while I tend to the horse," he said keeping hold of her hand and dropping to one knee so Cynthia could easily sit on the crude bench positioned by the fire. She nodded to him, tucking her cloak under her as she sat to protect herself from the cold air coming through the cracking wall. She lowered her head and sat perfectly still.

He'd seen men after a battle like this; stunned, overcome by the brutes they had to become to survive the fray. Warmth, food and rest had cured them and he hoped it would be the same with her.

Outside Constantine's horse sniffed out a patch of grass. Constantine waited until he raised his head and then led him to a small stream running nearby. Impatiently he lingered until the horse drank his fill after which Constantine led him back to the chapel and tied the reins to a nearby tree.

Inside he found Cynthia on her knees, face upturned, hands clasped in prayer. As quietly as he could, he walked to her side. There, for a moment, he thought he inhaled the scent of spring itself as the fire warmed her and brought color to her cheeks.

Silently, he stared at her, enjoying what the firelight revealed. Her cheeks were round and full, her face delicate. Hair, the color rich like golden coins, curled around her face like a halo. He moved closer and reached out, never touching her but tracing the curve of her head with his hands.

She sensed his presence and turned toward him. His breath caught when their gazes locked, her eyes so wide and clear that he thought he was looking into the clear pools of a bottomless lake. Tears no longer filled her eyes although sadness still left its imprint on them. Despite the depth of her grief, he knew from their first encounter that she was a strong woman, no wilting flower like many of the maidens in the court of Camelot. When she lifted her chin to catch his gaze more fully, he realized that he was staring and turned away.

He busied himself stoking the fire and the glow further illuminated the room. Alone in the woods with a beautiful and vulnerable woman, Constantine suspected that if his brother, Braedan, knew of this plight, he surely would have words of warning to say to him. Of his four brothers, Braeden, the oldest, joined the Knights of Camelot with Constantine, the other two seeking their futures elsewhere.

Since taking the vow, Braeden thought only of duty and honor. *Staring at a maiden like that will only cause her father to think you have said words of love and possibly stained her virtue,* Braeden would have said. *Nothing you can say will erase the sight of the tear-stained face of a daughter as you deny such deeds. Knights must be mindful of their duties and of their honor.*

Constantine poked at the fire with one of the damp sticks lying nearby. It wasn't that he did not realize the burden placed when he swore his sword to Arthur. Arthur was a great king and a good man. But if a beautiful woman led him astray, he reasoned, he would be forgiven. Surely others had done worse and were treated mercifully by the king.

He turned back in time to see Cynthia cross herself, her praying done. She rose and squared her shoulders.

"Sir knight," Cynthia said, clearly trying to keep her emotions smooth and remember her manners. "My behavior in front of a stranger was appalling indeed. Accept my apologies for that, and return to your quest." She extended her hand to him. "I have taken up far too much of your time and the King's."

Constantine bowed smoothly and took her hand, pressing his lips to the soft skin he found there. “I am a Knight of Arthur. I am honor bound to assist.”

“Your duty was to deliver the sad news of Sir William. And that you have done. Your task is complete.”

“It seems not,” he replied, the arch of his brow showing his concern. “The depth of pain and concern for your people tells me more needs to be done here in Leyborne shire.”

“William is...” she closed her eyes, the struggle to find the right words apparent on her face, “...was a good man. We will grieve him and deal with the aftermath. You need not take on this mantle.”

Constantine looked at her. Pain filled her eyes. Not physical pain, he knew, but the pain of what lay ahead. With that, he could help. “Ease your mind, Lady Cynthia. Even as William faced his end, he thought only of you. Stay, lady, for I have something to give you.”

As Constantine left her side, Cynthia closed her eyes and raised her face to heaven. Sir Constantine was a knight, a man of whom troubadours sang songs of deeds and honor. If he were half as noble as the songs she’d heard claimed knights to be, he would take serious note of her plight. A knight was less safe among the traitors and collaborators at Leyborne than was she.

Conflicted thoughts filled her. For the first time since William left, she felt truly alone.

Constantine returned. “If you would care to refresh yourself.” He handed her a wineskin. “Filled with local drink at the inn this morning.”

Cynthia took it and drank. The sweet, watered wine coursed through her, warming her and clearing her mind. She lowered the skin and saw Constantine staring at her again. In the firelight, she could see wariness in his eyes.

"Why did William not take you as his wife before he pledged his sword to Arthur? Such arranged marriages are preformed at any age."

She put down the skin. "Because William was a noble man. I was a child when I moved into the castle. He would not think to wed someone so young and naïve about the ways of the marriage bed. He wanted to wait until such time as I could understand more fully what a husband expects of his wife. But after he and my father left for Camelot on my tenth birthday, he came back once; to return the body of my father to his home. There was no time for a wedding as William left directly afterward."

"While William did indeed sit at the table, I know not your father." The guardedness in Constantine's eyes became more marked.

Cynthia pressed her lips together. "My father did not have the skills to become a knight, though he would lead me to believe otherwise. When I learned that my father rode only as William's steward, I vowed to never shatter his dream by letting him know that I knew the truth."

Constantine arched his brows, his expression flickering.

"A child left to her own means ages rapidly," Cynthia explained. "The pyre released my father from his living lie, and, with it, me from my burden to bear it. Now I beg you mercy, sir. I will not dishonor whatever remains of his legacy by speaking freely of his failures in his death."

"Then so be it," Constantine agreed. "The matter concerns me not." He held out his hand. "But I vowed to deliver William's last will and testament and I do that now." He opened his fingers and heard her gasp. "By the crest on this ring, all the lands and everything William owned are now yours."

She eyed him somberly as the silence hung between them. With a shaking hand she took the ring from him and held it tightly to her chest. In a moment no longer than a heartbeat, the pain she felt suddenly turned to hope.

Her guise steeled. She thrust the ring deep into the pocket of her tunic. "You said you vowed to help William, did you not?"

He nodded. "Aye."

"By a knight's honor, tell me now, can you refuse anything I ask?"

"By a knight's honor I am bound to assist any who require help," he returned.

"In any manner?"

"In any way possible to resolve the plight."

"What I ask is not the usual. Are you prepared to hear it?"

Constantine saw hope rise in her eyes. Knowing there could be no reply but one, he drew in a breath and bowed. "What will you require of me, lady?"

The ruins appeared to go silent as if around them nature held its breath. The moment seemed to go on forever until finally he heard her voice, soft and deliberate. "I'd ask then that you marry me."

Chapter Five

At her words, Constantine took a step backward in shock and confusion. Did he hear her right or did his mind, burdened by the weight of the task he assumed play a trick on him?

"Why?" he asked, his heartbeat rising.

"Because my father is dead and so is the man who would be my husband and Lord of this land. Because a tyrannical monster now lives in the manor, his evil stench permeating the shire and everything in it. When he learns of the grave news you have delivered to me this day, his hold on the shire and its people will be complete," Cynthia answered as calmly as she could though inside every emotion ran wild. "Even if I could record William's will, which I cannot, without a husband, the lands will be forfeit."

"The Bishop will uphold William's bequest," Constantine countered.

"The Bishop has fled, along with most of the holy men. Only Friar Joseph, who keeps this chapel open for any who wish to still call upon the Almighty for help, stays to endure Simon's wrath and rule." Unable to weather his piercing gaze, Cynthia glanced away. "You are strong and powerful, a Knight of Arthur. No one will dispute your declaration." She took a breath and met his gaze once more. "With a husband I can protect my people as I have tried to do all these long years with William gone."

Constantine stood silent. When Arthur girded him as a knight, he vowed to protect all women, but not in this way.

"Nay, Lady. I cannot. Honor was one thing; marriage another. You deserve to wed someone of your own choosing for love not duty."

Cynthia's shoulders slumped and she turned away from him. "Then all is lost."

"Take heart. I will send out a call and Camelot will answer. William's lands will be restored and his bequest honored," he promised her.

She folded her arms across her stomach and turned back to him. "I fear your ride will be futile. If word of William's death reaches the shire before the knights arrive, Simon will claim to Leyborne Castle and the lands that make up the shire. Once he does, he will never relinquish it, not even to Arthur."

"Then I must make sure your claim is filed before Simon can proclaim himself as Sovereign," he said, his voice colored with a mixture of sorrow for her plight and anticipation for her providence. He stepped to her and placed his hands on her shoulders. His fingers buried themselves in her long blond tresses. The warmth of her skin infused his thoughts and drove away all thoughts of warring to focus only on her.

The pull of attraction welled inside him. A dangerous feeling he carefully controlled in the past, he felt strangely beset by its intensity for this woman. Some knights embraced the tender emotion that suddenly gripped his heart. Some even wrote songs and sonnets about it. But not knights like him;

knights who made their way alone in the world and shed ties that would bind them to what could be lost.

At least not until now. Drawn to Cynthia like a moth to the flame, he felt his strength of mind begin to dissolve just touching her.

What had William been thinking to leave this woman unprotected and his heritage in such disarray that a man could simply ride in and claim it all? To follow Arthur, William left a girl, young and untouched. But in his absence she had grown into a woman; a strong woman who protected his people in his absence using her intelligence and cunning while she waited for his return to fulfill a contract struck but not of her choosing.

As beautiful as she was brave, as strong as she was gentle, Cynthia would have no lack of suitors once it became known that William was dead. No doubt Lord Simon wanted to make sure Cynthia would be his long before either news of William's return or demise reached back to Leyborne shire.

With gentle pressure, he urged Cynthia to turn to him. He meant to tell her that she would be safe, that he would protect her at all costs, but no words would come. Instead he rested his forehead on hers and curled a hand around her waist.

"Lady, I fear I dishonor William by what stirs in my heart," he said, his hand moving up her back.

"What are you doing?" she whispered in response to his arms tightening around her.

"Something I should not," he said. His breathing hitched as he inhaled the lavender that had been rinsed into her hair. "Not now, maybe not ever, but I am powerless to stop."

"Is it evil?" she asked in anticipation. Her hand moved to rest upon his chest. "I can feel your heart race."

"Nay, 'tis a natural thing. I am going to kiss you." He gave her no chance to protest but covered her mouth with his. Her lips were warm and soft against his mouth, and after a few moments, he felt her melt into him.

As Constantine kissed her, Cynthia felt as though a mischievous sprite suddenly possessed her, but she did not care. Heat rose inside her and she responded to the gentle pressure of his lips. She should not be doing this, she thought, but reason fast slipped away. She could do no more than enjoy the way she felt in his arms and allow him to kiss her more completely than she ever dreamed a man could.

She felt his tongue trace the seam of her lips and she tensed.

"Open your mouth, Cynthia," he whispered.

When she did, he slid his tongue inside. Like a practiced musician, his tongue played upon hers, caressing, evoking awareness and feelings. Cynthia felt her heart slam against her chest. Cautiously she answered his strokes with some gentle explorations of her own.

He pressed his body more deeply into hers and she tried to stop back, but his strong arms would not allow it. She could only stay willingly imprisoned in his arms enjoying the new feelings his kiss stirred inside her.

A building sensation ripened between her legs, growing more intense with each stroke of Constantine's tongue inside her mouth. As the awareness of man and woman grew, Cynthia began to move her hips in tune to the thrusting of Constantine's tongue. When she realized how she was responding to him, she stiffened.

"I do not understand these feelings inside me," she said pulling away from him.

He pulled her gently back. "No," he whispered against her lips, "'tis natural what you are feeling. The want of man for woman and woman for man should not be denied."

"But I should be doing no more than preparing to mourn William," Cynthia said. "These thoughts I have, these things I feel, are sinful."

Constantine stroked her hair. "Not sinful, milady. Wonderful and natural, especially in the dawning of womanhood."

"But perhaps they should not be stirred in the setting of grief," Cynthia countered.

Constantine kissed her forehead. "Milady, as your experiences grow, you will come to understand that feelings such as these do not follow rules made by man." He tipped her chin to him. "Attraction and its consequences do not follow any system of logic."

"But attraction is not love," she said, her eyes on his moist lips. "And love must govern my body."

Constantine smiled. "I think you will find it harder to hold fast to that vow as you discover the joys of your womanhood."

When his kisses returned, the gentleness of discovery replaced with passion, hard, demanding, and unrelenting. She felt a awareness flow through her like a spreading fire, igniting a yearning she had only before imagined.

She knew about love; the kind of love for father and daughter, even the kind of love she felt for William. But her attraction to Constantine was different. More powerful, harder to control, more intense than anything she ever felt before. She wanted to go on feeling the way he made her feel at this moment forever. She wrapped her arms around his neck and accepted the gift he gave her. When his hand left her waist and touched her breast, she inhaled sharply and nearly jumped out of her skin.

In reaction, Constantine broke off the kiss. His smile appeared both striking and apologetic. "I fear, milady, that demons have possessed me after all. I have indeed overstepped my vow of chivalry and have sinned in this most holy place."

Cynthia took a few steps backward and put a hand to her lips. Her fingertips found them moist and puffy. Warmth lingered from the heat of his kisses. She stared at him. He was so devastatingly handsome that she could imagine women putting themselves in peril just to have him save them and see him smile. It took a moment for her swirling mind to focus on his words. When she finally understood what he had said, she felt heat rise on her cheeks.

"Then I, too, have sinned. I should have not kissed you. I was to be married."

"But you are not."

"And I've taken no suitors since the arrangement, so I am a virgin."

"Then I pray that I will be the first to show you what can be if and when you will allow it," he said boldly, stepping closer to her.

As he took her in his arms, he saw her look over his shoulder, her eyes reacting to a presence she saw there. A moment later, he felt first a hard object strike his head and then pain explode inside it. Instinctively his hand went to the hilt of the sword in the scabbard at his waist, but another blow followed. Dazed, he stumbled backward a step before turning around.

He heard Cynthia scream and blinked hard to try to clear the stupor that had formed inside his head. He wobbled, found his balance and took a step toward the attacker.

"No!" Cynthia positioned her body in front of Constantine.

"Lady," he said trying to steady his wobbly legs as colors danced before his eyes. "Stand behind me." Despite the throbbing at the base of his skull, somehow he managed to change positions with her. With both hands he pulled the sword free and raised it in defense. He shook his head and willed his vision to clear.

Slowly the form focused in front of him. Not an outlaw outfitted in armor ready for war stood there, but a portly holy man, dressed in dark sackcloth tied with a length of rope. In the monk's hand was the metal cross that just moments before stood on the crumbling altar one corner marred now with what Constantine knew had to be his blood.

Again Cynthia stood between them. "Friar Joseph, I am in no danger." With gentle pressure on his hand, she urged Constantine to lower his sword. "Get some water so we can tend to this man's wound," she said to the monk.

The friar looked from her face to Constantine's before returning the relic to the altar. Then crossing himself, he hurried out of the chapel to comply.

Cynthia put an arm around Constantine's waist and led him to the remains of a hand-carved wooden pew. "You must forgive Friar Joseph. He only meant to protect me." She took the sword from his hand and set it on the altar near the cross. "How do you feel?"

Constantine pressed his palm to his head. "Like I rode full tilt into a stone wall." He closed his eyes as Cynthia searched his head for the wound. He winced when she found it.

"Try to be still," she said, parting his hair with her fingers to expose the cut. "Although it bleeds, it's not very deep. I thank the Almighty that Friar Joseph is not all that strong."

"Strong enough," Constantine replied, wincing again as Cynthia continued searching for any other injury.

"Still yourself, sir," Cynthia said. "I need to see if the second blow opened another wound." As his hair slid over the back of her hand, Cynthia could only akin the feeling to silk cloth sliding over her skin. She felt her cheeks warm when she realized she enjoyed the feeling far too much.

"Ow," Constantine said as her fingers returned to his wound. "It seems you draw a champion as easily as I draw a breath. First a contingent of men in the woods and now a holy man in his crumbling church." More curious than ever about the golden haired, blue-eyed angel who now cradled his chin with her hands, he marveled silently once again at her strength and conviction despite the harsh circumstances into which she had been thrust.

"Friar Joseph stayed behind after Lord Simon's men ransacked the monastery and took everything that could bring a price at market," she replied, her fingers drifting to his temples. She saw a scar mar the skin over his right eye and another run jagged near his ear and wondered how he might have come to get them. Her fingers trailed a slow path to his cheeks. "Do you hurt elsewhere?"

She couldn't help herself; she ran her hands down his neck and across his shoulders. The body beneath her fingertips proclaimed him a fighting man. Without breaking contact with him, she sat down next to him, trailing one hand across his chest while the other stayed firmly on his shoulder. He felt like a rock hard masterpiece carved from marble. She stirred restlessly as she touched him, all sorts of thoughts racing through her. She felt him tense as her touch continued lower, to the firm rippling muscles of his stomach. Did someone who loved him touch him like this, she wondered? A paramour? A wife perhaps? Could that be why he turned down her shameless proposal of marriage?

She saw his eyes soften. Without breaking his gaze, he took her hand in his and brought it to his lips. "I fear I am about to sin once more," he said softly. He leaned closer to her, "unless you stop me now."

Almost shyly, she shook her head. "I do not wish to."

Their lips touched, meshing together as though paired by the angels themselves. Shivers ran up Cynthia's spine when Constantine's hand roamed her back. A small sigh escaped her mouth as she surrendered to the sensations tumbling one against the other.

He kissed her eyes, her mouth, her cheeks, her chin, as though he could not get enough of her. Cynthia caught his lips in short, quick kisses that left her breathless.

"What are you thinking?" he said, when he again broke the kiss, the words whispered against her lips.

"That you're very good at seduction and I am wicked to have succumbed when I should be in mourning." Cynthia blushed and looked away, glad he could not read her thoughts. This sudden attraction she felt for him did not lessen the urgency of what needed to be done. "Forgive me," she said rising. "You should not think that all the women of this shire are so bold."

"There is nothing to forgive," he assured, his smile wide and dazzling.

Cynthia felt his gaze sweep over her and drew in a shaky breath as she felt every inch of skin on her body warm. What was wrong with her? The pulsing sensation between her legs her grew steadily even though he only looked at her. His bold assessment of her body raised bumps on her skin and heat on her breasts, stoking the fire he masterfully ignited inside her by his kiss.

"Lady Cynthia, are you all right?"

Friar Joseph's voice brought some sense back to her.

"I'm fine," she replied, rising and taking a step away from Constantine. She took the bucket of water and cloth from the monk's hands. "But I can't say the same for Sir Constantine. The lump on his scalp compares to the size of a goose egg and I imagine a pain inside his head will be hard to tolerate."

Friar Joseph wrung his hands. "Sir Constantine? A knight?" He raised his eyes and crossed himself again. "The saints forgive me. I almost killed him."

Constantine rose on shaky legs. "It will take more than a knock on the head to kill me, Friar." A fresh stab of pain sent blinding light into his eyes and he felt himself sway. Friar Joseph quickly strode to him and looped the knight's arm across his shoulder for support.

"Rest here, Sir Constantine," Cynthia said as the monk settled Constantine down in the pew. "Friar Joseph will accompany me back to Leyborne Castle and return with some salve and one of my handmaiden's herbal concoctions to help ease the pain in your head. In the morning, you must leave here. It is not safe for a knight alone among traitors and mercenaries."

"Then truly it must be equally dangerous for you," he replied.

"Safe enough for me for the time. But if Lord Simon discovered a Knight of Arthur here in the shire, he would not stop until he killed you, along with anyone who gave you aid."

"I will not leave you to the whim of a madman," Constantine protested.

"You have no choice. For both our sakes." Without waiting for an answer, she turned and left the chapel.

"Friar, talk to her. Tell her the folly of her decision," Constantine said, looking past the monk.

Friar Joseph shook his head. "Lady Cynthia knows what is best for her people. She has always been strong willed. I will be back anon and then you must be on your way." He walked to the doorway and then stopped. He turned back to Constantine and raised his hand. "May God protect you on your way back to Camelot," he said extending a blessing to Constantine. "For no one here will preserve should you be discovered."

Chapter Six

The sun already set by the time Cynthia returned. Lord Simon was already back from Donahyde Castle. Light spilled from the window of his bedroom. Strange, she thought. Simon did not relish long rides and normally stayed the night as a guest of Mordred. As she rode into the courtyard, she tried not to look at the faces of the guards patrolling there and call attention to herself.

The stable boy ran to take her horse. "His Lordship been asking for you."

"What did you tell him?" Cynthia asked as she handed her mare to the stable boy.

"That I knew nothing."

"Did he chide you?"

"Not much, my lady."

The boy's forehead creased with worry. Cynthia suspected that he had been deprived his supper because of her. She reached into her pocket and pulled out a coin. "After you rub down the mare, go you to the back door of the inn and give this to the innkeeper's wife," she said placing it in the boy's hand. "She will wrap you some bread and meat."

The boy nodded. "Best go in through the kitchen, milady. At this hour you can make the stairs without being seen."

Cynthia lifted the hood of her cape over her head and quickly walked away. The cook and some maids busied themselves with cleaning up after the evening meals and she found it easy to slip through the kitchen unnoticed. While she climbed the back stairs to her chamber, she thought about Constantine.

Even now she could almost feel his lips on hers. She brought her hand to her neck, her skin still warm from his touch, and marveled on how well she fit into the hard contours of his battled toned body.

She could not imagine why a man like him did not have a paramour or wife waiting for him. Yet it seemed he did not by the way he kissed her. A smile curled her lips, but quickly faded when she realized the next time she may see him might be as he battled with Simon to free the shire. She did not wish to think about the danger surrounding his conviction to help her.

She made it to her room and breathed a prayer of thanksgiving to whatever saints helped her. There Jane waited, worry lines creasing her brow.

“Lord Simon has been looking for you.”

“I imagine so,” Cynthia said biting her lip. She put her hand into the pocket of her tunic and retrieved the ring. She held it out. “William is dead.”

Jane put her hand over the ring as if to hide it. “How?”

“Fallen in battle.”

“No courier rode to court today,” Jane said, disbelief in her tone. “How do you know this?”

Cynthia curled her fingers back around the ring. “A Knight of Arthur brought the terrible news to me this day.”

“A knight? Here? Does his lordship know?”

Cynthia looked over her shoulder as though looking for a spy. “Nay, and he must never know it. Sir Constantine has sent word to Camelot for more knights to come and free us of our terrible plight. Until then we must act as though William still lives.” She leveled her gaze at Jane. “Can you do this?”

Jane nodded. “Aye. To have the devil that settled here exorcised, I will do whatever I must. But the fact remains, his lordship waits for you.”

Cynthia walked to the clothes chest and put the ring deep inside among the fine fabrics there. “I must not keep him waiting much longer.”

Cynthia’s mind drifted again to Constantine as Jane helped her into a dress. As Jane brushed her hair Cynthia imagined Constantine’s fingers tangling in her curls. She imagined how he would channel his strength to tenderness when his hand would cup her cheek preparing her for his kiss. She closed her eyes and tried to envision what their first night together might bring. Would he be as tender as the touch she felt at the monastery, or would he let loose his power and ravage her?

She felt heat creep across her cheeks. How wicked of her to think of these things. She never thought about men like that before. William was to have been her husband and her first. For all these many years he had never even kissed her. And no man of court or visiting Lord ever drew her fancy. Until now.

Jane parted Cynthia’s hair and let it flow down her back. “Your cheeks are rosy and there’s a sparkle in your eyes. Did something happen to please you, my lady?” She handed Cynthia a mirror.

"Riding at night invigorates me," Cynthia returned. She looked at her reflection. Simon must not see what Jane had.

Cynthia rose, composing herself for Simon's interrogation. How long it would be would depend entirely based on how well she would lie to him.

"Take a poultice of your healing herbs to Friar Joseph. He waits for you just beyond the entrance to the forest beyond the North Tower. He requires your salve to heal the knight's wounds. Then wait for me in chamber," Cynthia said. "Best I see Lord Simon alone."

****

Simon waited for her in the oriel behind the Great Hall. A large room with a fireplace and many books, William, a scholar by nature, had it built as a place of learning. When Cynthia came to the castle, he instructed his own tutor to educate her in the same manner in which he had learned mathematics, reading, philosophy and the like. Before Lord Simon turned it into his war room, she spent many happy days with her instructor and many happier nights teaching Jane in secret by candlelight what she had learned by day. But now as she entered, the room seemed more like a prison than a library.

He stood next to the fire, his hands clasped behind his back. "You just returned?"

Cynthia lowered her head. "I felt the need to pray at the monastery."

His right arm shot out. "Your need 'tis why the chapel still stands, but I warn you, lady, do not test my tolerance."

Cynthia felt her temper rise and struggled to keep her voice even. "It barely maintains its standing as a holy place. Your men have looted the altar and defiled the church hall."

"Rumor," Simon said, dismissing the acquisition. "Perhaps the chapel falls in ruin from time and neglect."

"But is holy ground still and I needed to confess to a priest," Cynthia replied not wanting to prolong her meeting with him by engaging in a battle of words she could not win.

Simon lowered his arm and walked to her. "I could have sent for Friar Joseph if you felt the need for a confessor." He reached out and took a blond tendril of hair between his fingers before bringing it to his nose and inhaling deeply its aroma. "And what sin did you confess? Anger? Pride?" He let loose of her hair and circled her, his gaze roaming down the length of her body. "Perhaps you grow restless in your solitude." He ran a hand up her arm and let his fingers linger for a moment on her collarbone. "Perhaps you feel the want of desire stir within you." He stepped closer to her. "Or Lust?"

She met his gaze and held her ground. "Since my sin has been forgiven, I have none to tell you."

"You are past twenty years. Do you not crave the affection of a man and the feel of a child in your belly?"

Cynthia's heart skipped. Before meeting Constantine, the question would not have set her aback. The feelings he stirred inside her eclipse any that she felt before. The basic need to feel these things grew inside her now just by thinking of him. But the awful news he brought with him evoked equally compelling feelings and she would play the role of betrothed as long as she could. "All that I will have when William returns."

Simon grabbed her shoulders. "Tis folly to wait for a man who cares more about the quest than his home and the comfort of a woman."

"I vowed to save myself for him and it is a vow I intend to keep."

"A vow as such will make you an old hag before a bride."

"Then a hag I shall be."

Simon pulled her to him. "I grow weary of this game. I have taken almost all that was William's, there is but one prize left."

He began to lower his mouth to hers when Cynthia put her hand on his chest and pushed away. "I refuse this." He tried to kiss her again but she turned her head. "You can try to take by force what will never be yours, and although you may succeed in owning my body, my heart will never yield,"

He saw Cynthia's face fill with such contempt that it chilled him to the bone. He pushed her away and pointed to the door. "Leave me."

She began to hurry away when he voice stopped her. "Think on this carefully, Cynthia." He waited until she turned fully to him before speaking. "My patience grows thin and your time out of my bed grows short." His eyes darkened with barely checked anger. "The next time you pray it would be wise to pray to your saints that when that time does come, I will be as tolerant as I am this day."

Cynthia turned and ran to her solar. She knew she did not have much time before the news of William's death would reach Simon. Her heart ached, but she held fast to Constantine's plan. The knights would come. They must.

Saints help me, she prayed. If Arthur's knights did not come in time, she may indeed have to yield and become Simon's wife to save the people.

****

He had to see her.

Constantine sat at the back table in the inn and drained the goblet of its wine. Although Cynthia pleaded with him to leave, by his vow of honor, he could not abandon her.

He sent Friar Joseph to Camelot to bring his brother and his fellow knights back to restore William's lands. While he waited for them, he would protect Cynthia as best he could from the evil warlord who took possession of the castle, the shire, and everything around it for miles.

His fingers tightened around the stem of the cup. A few well-placed questions and some better-placed coins had garnered him a fair picture of her plight.

Simon ruled like a Saxon; blood and death his means of justice to all those opposing him. The alliance he forged with Mordred with the promise of his forces the ride to Camelot to confront Arthur afforded Simon a degree of protection and ability to govern the people with fear and an iron fist. That might play well into Constantine's plans, for if all went accordingly, the battle would be engaged here in surprise giving the advantage to Arthur's knights. Though Constantine's initial charge was freeing Cynthia, vanquishing Mordred before he could strike at Arthur would be a sweet adjunct.

Cynthia. What about her affected him so? William spoke not much of her giving Constantine nothing to envision and no reason to think her fair. But what he found when he saw her was beauty surpassed any that had tempted him in the past. Though he would have needed to be blind not to be captivated by her comely face, her innocence captivated him even as her strength seduced. She seemed freshening unaware of her womanliness and it was clear to him that she had not yet explored it. At first her kiss tested, just the hesitant touch of lips. When he showed her there could be more, she responded with the beginning of a passion he knew he could ignite.

Another time, he would have finished what started in the ruins of the monastery instead of holding back. But he gave William his solemn vow and he could not recant it. He lived by a code of honor and he would fill his pledge, giving Cynthia all William possessed as he wanted and the ability to choose someone with whom to share it.

The shuffle of feet coming closer caught his attention and he looked up from the table at which he sat.

"Strangers invite questions," said a burly man who slid onto the bench opposite him.

"So it seems," Constantine replied.

"If you insist on remaining in the shire, they'll be more."

"Let me ask you one, then," Constantine said.

"And it be?"

"Your name."

"Why?" the man asked, wariness in his eyes.

"To know the name of the name I would drink with."

The man hesitated before giving a one word answer. "Ranulf."

Constantine signaled to the barmaid. "Another," he said pointing to his goblet, "and one for my friend, Ranulf, here."

"I'll take the wine, but not the friendship," Ranulf said, placing both his hands on the table. "Friendships with strangers invite death. The lord's men patrol for poachers and deliver the lord's form of justice on the spot." He made a fist and ran his thumb across his neck in a cutting motion.

"I come naught for friendships," Constantine returned, nodding at the barmaid who brought the wine. "I come for work."

Ranulf downed the wine in a few gulps and then swiped his hand across his mouth. "Work, eh? I heard your song last night. It be passable." He looked Constantine. "But you have a soldier's bearing." His gaze settled on Constantine's forehead. "And a soldier's scar."

"Discharged from the army," Constantine quickly assured. "I seek another profession."

"Best you seek to better yourself somewhere else."

"Not soon. I used the last of my pay to buy the wine."

Ranulf stood, his eyes judging Constantine. Then he nodded. "Suit yourself, but it would be a pity to have that that pretty face of yours covered in burial mud.

"Aye," Constantine said, his gaze holding firm. "A great pity indeed."

Chapter Seven

The keep of Leyborne Castle appeared alive with the sounds of the merchants. Twice during each cycle of the moon, Simon allowed them to set up shop in and around the castle grounds to trade and sell their wares. For this privilege, he took what he wanted and collected a heavy tax on final tallies. The merchants, however, still made a profit because they could sell their goods directly to the public, without intervention of those who bought for resale, raising prices or lowering quality and quantity. For this reason, they endured the contingencies.

In the courtyard young boys busily hammered together some temporary stalls for arriving merchants as groups of young girls watched, each hoping to capture some attention. Smoke wafted skyward from fires over which cooked varieties of food for sale. Nobles and their ladies decorated themselves with all manner of fine trappings and haggled with sellers for the best prices. And all around jugglers began impromptu performances for those who gathered to watch.

Cynthia and Jane roamed among the villagers, stopping at one table or another to look at the yards of material for dresses and ribbons, and baubles for adornments.

"I do love it when the merchants come," Cynthia said, accepting a handful of flowers from a woman selling bread and cheese. "I feel hidden from Simon for a time."

"Can we find the goldsmith?" Jane asked. "I like to look at the earbobs he makes." A smile crept up on her lips. "I think his apprentice has taken a liking to me. Perhaps he will give me a pair he crafts just for me." She tucked a dark strand of hair behind one ear. "I still wear the ones my mother used to pierce my earlobes. A change would be nice."

"I do envy you," Cynthia replied, seeing the sunlight catch the gold circles on Jane's ears. "My father would naught let me do that. He feared I'd develop an infection from the piercing and perish."

Jane laughed. "A healing salve of comfrey would ensure that does not happen."

Cynthia grabbed Jane's hand and pulled her behind a large stacking of hay. "'Tis not wise to let someone hear you speak of the old ways," she warned. "Lord Simon holds to no religion."

"Better a druid than a barbarian," Jane said, her voice hardening.

"Better alive than dead," Cynthia corrected. "Your elixirs and potions have helped many."

Jane began to respond, but Cynthia put a hand on her shoulder and stopped her. Around the corner came Constantine, fingering a lute and singing a song of a knight's deeds. He saw her and stopped but continued to sing. Though villagers soon surrounded him, he looked passed them at her, making her feel as though he sang just for her.

She walked to him. "You have a good voice," she said, her gaze resting on his mouth as he finished the song. No other words came. She could only think of his kisses. Her gaze dropped to his fingers on the strings and could think only of his touch.

"I've been told I'm a little heavy-handed with the strings," he replied.

"Whoever told you that knew little. 'Tis only your song that is heavy," she replied. She gave the flowers to Jane and extended her hand. "Perhaps I could teach you something lighter." Constantine nodded and handed her the instrument. She ran her fingers lightly over the wood. "Could be a fine instrument. You should have taken care with it." She held it out to him,

He took it back from her. "A friend wanted me to have it." He saw her face cloud and realized she thought it may be a lady who gave it to him. To keep up the ruse for anyone listening, Constantine could not tell her that he took it from a back room at the inn where it had been rudely discarded.

"A song, Lady," someone from the crowd cried out.

"Yes, a song," another agreed.

"A duet," a third shouted, handing Cynthia a similar instrument.

Soon the two voices became many. Cynthia nodded first to the throng and then to Constantine. She walked to a nearby bench and sat. She started to play a wistful tune.

Constantine intended to try to join her in the song, but when she began to sing, there seemed to be magic in her voice. As if rapt by the song of a siren, he could not take his eyes from her. Her face lit as though the sun shone on it alone on it. She took such joy in the music. The crowd stilled and seemed as captivated as he.

He ached to reach out and touch her cheek to see if it felt as smooth as it looked. His body began to long for the feel of hers. His mind conjured up a vision of his fingers tangling in her hair while he kissed her rosy mouth. Waves of longing crashed through him and he barely managed to reign in the urge to take her in his arms and act upon every desire that grew within him.

She looked up from the strings and tilted her head to him. His breath caught when his gaze met hers. Her eyes were so clear, so full of life, so inviting. He wanted nothing more than to be able to lose himself inside their deep blue depths.

She turned briefly away as some of the villagers called her name, momentarily breaking the bond. He knew he had to somehow control the notions that filled his mind if he were to carry out this guise. He took up his own instrument and began to play and follow her tune. In minutes his fingers moved as lightly on the strings as hers.

She turned back to him, smiling as she sang. When his fingers fumbled over the strings, she threw back her head and lightly laughed, a gesture he found all too beguiling.

"Come Therefore Now, My Gentle Fere," Cynthia said as she continued to strum the lute. "Do you know it?'

He nodded. His mother sang the song often and he developed a memory for the music and words. He hoped he would not be as inept as he felt and began to sing. Soon her voice joined his.

"Come therefore now, my gentle fere, whom as my heart I hold full dear..."

He tried not to look her as their voices blended, the song continuing, soft and intimate. But as the song drew to a close, he found he could not look away.

"*I cannot live without thee, sweet. Time bids us now our love complete.*"

Their eyes held and he reached out and touched her face. His fingers caressed her cheek to let her know that he sung the words just for her. As he suspected her skin felt like rose petals and he began to lean toward her when suddenly a series of slow, deliberate claps echoed in the courtyard. Before he could move, Cynthia bolted to standing and backed away, her eyes filling with dread.

"I seem to have interrupted a most charming moment." The tone in the voice simmered with anger. "Please do go on."

Cynthia took another step backward. "Nay, you did not, my Lord," she said as Simon approached. "I was simply enjoying the song."

Simon looked from Cynthia to Constantine. "Indeed you were."

Constantine bowed. "Do not blame the lady. She felt obligated to be kind to a stranger, no more."

Simon glowered at the dispersing throng. "I see." He reached a hand out to Cynthia. "You should accompany me inside."

Constantine sprang between them. "Milord, pardon my manners. I am Constantine, minstrel extraordinaire and looking for work."

"You'll find none here," Simon said, glaring. He pressed his hand out again and waited until Cynthia took it. "Come, my dear. It's time to go."

Constantine could do no more than watch her leave. He knew if he went after her, he would tip his hand. Hopelessly outnumbered by the soldiers in the courtyard, he could not risk a confrontation with Simon. He had no way of knowing how long it would take the Friar to reach Camelot or whether he even would. For now, he would have to bide his time and make contingency plans if Friar Joseph failed.

But he would find a way to see Cynthia again this day. That he did know.

****

The door to the castle kitchen shook, as the pounding on hit grew more intense. The cook wiped her hands on the white cloth tied around her waist.

"I'm coming. I'm coming." She threw back the bolt and yanked the door open. "What be so important that you nearly take down the door with your fist?" she asked to the man she found there.

He brushed her aside with his large hand. "I be needing a word with the Lord." He took a step to her. "And I need it now."

"And just who should I tell him calls at this time of night?" the cook asked.

"Ranulf the stone carver. The lord knows me."

The cook looked up at the man looming over her. Darkness and danger lay deep in his eyes as if in warning. She feared the worst should she tell him to go away.

"Annie," she said to her apprentice stirring the stew that cooked in the hearth. "Tell the master that he has company." She looked into the man's eyes. A shiver ran up her spine at the emptiness she saw. "And be quick about it."

Chapter Eight

Finger's barely touching Simon's outstretched hand, Cynthia walked with him to her chamber. In the deathly quiet surrounding them, she dared not breathe for fear the sound of the air rushing from her lungs would sound like the clatter of armed men.

Simon had said nothing to her since leaving the courtyard. She knew she angered him, but she would not let him know how wary his silence made her.

"My dear, your hand feels like ice," he said, pausing at her chamber door and lowering his hand, leaving hers suspended in the air.

"The approaching eve holds a chill," Cynthia replied, turning to the door.

"The minstrel was ill-mannered."

She heard the anger in his voice and turned back to him. "How so, my lord?"

Simon clasped his hands behind his back. "He appeared prepared to take liberty with you. The idleness of court could make you the victim of vicious rumor."

"He got caught up in the festivities only, Sire. Nothing more."

Simon regarded her answer quizzically. "Your mouth professes your innocence, but your eyes do not."

She dropped her gaze for a fraction of a heartbeat and then regained his eyes. In them she saw the fire of building desire. She felt dread well inside her. She knew Simon could take her now, on the stone cold floor outside her chamber if he chose to do so. In the south tower and no one would hear her cries.

Not willing to let him know how close she was to panic, she lifted her chin, challenging him to make his move. "I hope you are not beginning to doubt the sincerity of my vow to William. I will not betray him."

"But he is dead."

His words made a cold chill run up Cynthia's spine. Did he know? "Why do you say such things?" she asked.

"Because he has not come back these long years and there has been no word from him. Surely by now a man with a pledge given for your hand would return home to seal the marriage." Simon's gaze roamed over Cynthia like a trader eyeing wares. "And partake of the marriage bed."

"Until I see his body, I will know no other man," Cynthia said with all the strength she could summon.

A rush of air left Simon's lips. "Of course not, my dear," he replied from behind clenched teeth. "And to that end I will demand an apology from the minstrel in full court."

"I know I have disturbed you, my Lord. For that, accept my apology now and let us be done with this incident." She softened her voice. "I will spend the night praying for both forgiveness and guidance."

Simon reached around her and opened her chamber door. "Then I suggest you hurry to begin." He took her by the arm and drove her inside. "Pray also that I don't lose control in the dark hours of night and come back." He tightened his grip on her arm. "The time fast approaches when neither saints nor sinners will keep me from you."

"A threat, my lord?" Cynthia asked, hoping her voice did not belie her worry with his words.

"No, my dear, a promise." Simon's mouth curved in a vicious grin as he reacted to the look of horror on Cynthia's face. He released her, spun on his heels and slammed the door behind him.

Even as Cynthia covered her ears, his ominous laughter resonated through the heavy door and echoed inside her head. She pressed her hands against her breast and raised her eyes. She would pray this night. For Constantine's safety in exchange for her own if need be.

****

Wearing a chamber robe over her white nightdress, Cynthia curled up in a chair and stared into the dying embers in the hearth. It was late; the castle long since locked down for the night. But sleep was far from her mind.

She lit another candle when the first one sputtered out. Would Simon make good on his threat? She hugged her knees with her arms, banishing the thought from her mind. She clung to the hope that in a few more days the Knights of Camelot would come and she would be free.

She smiled. Free then to finish what nearly started in the courtyard. Before Constantine she never thought of anything except marrying William. But William was dead and Constantine's kisses made her aware of what could be. If she would ever experience the passion of love, she knew it would be with him.

A noise in the corridor caught her attention. Fearing Simon had decided to come back, she picked up a heavy brass candlestick and walked to the door. Lifting it as high as she could with her right hand, she pulled the door open with her left.

Constantine stood on the threshold. He looked at her raised hand. "I see you do not need me to be safe this night."

Cynthia pulled him inside and closed the door. "Why have you come? 'Tis too dangerous."

"I couldn't help myself." He took the candlestick from her and placed it on the floor. "Since we met, you haunt my thoughts when we are apart"

Cynthia shied and looked down. "You tempt me so."

"And you tempt me." He lifted her chin with the tips of his fingers.

"Surely there have been other women who drew your interest."

"None like you." He maneuvered until her back touched the wall, then leaned into her. He rested his forehead against hers. "Kiss me," he urged. Even before the words were out, his hands clasped Cynthia's head and dragged her mouth to his.

He kissed her like she had never been kissed before. The fierce wildness of his mouth on hers was like a possession that set fire to her blood. His hands moved down her spine and, grasping her hips, he pulled her closer. How easily she slid into the hard curves of his body.

He pulled his mouth away, his gaze holding hers. "Cynthia," he whispered, huskiness in his tone.

"I came to Leyborne shire only to deliver terrible news, but I find now I came to also lose my heart. I have not the right to assume you feel the same."

Cynthia's gaze roamed his face. Moonlight coming in from the balcony painted him in silver and the flickering shadows from the movement of clouds crossing the light made him seem haloed like an angel. He stood perfectly still waiting, yet she could feel every muscle tremble.

"But I do."

She did not know if she spoke it or thought it. But it did not matter. This is what she had been waiting for, hoping for. She was not meant to lose her heart to William; she knew that now. She was meant to surrender to Constantine.

She traced his lips with her fingertips. His mouth formed in a kiss against them so light, so gentle, yet it sent a fire though her.

"What are we to do?" she asked him.

"My brother and the other knights will come soon."

Cynthia felt the ice-cold rush of fear replace the warmth inside her as she remembered Simon's threat-veiled promise. "And if they do not?"

"Another vow I make now." He caught her hand in his and pressed a kiss against the soft skin at her wrist. "With or without Arthur's knights, your people will be free of the tyrant who now controls the shire." His free hand drifted to her shoulder and he traced the soft line of her neck with his fingertips. "And you will be free to choose the man who would be your husband."

Cynthia had time to watch his lips part, notice the soft curl of his hair as it brushed his neck and the way his dark lashes shadowed his cheeks as his eyes closed before his lips touched hers. She swayed to meet him, her hands clasping around his neck. All the fears tugging at the edges of her mind ceased to exist replaced by the heat of his kiss.

Suddenly she pulled back. “Did you hear that?”

“What?” Constantine asked, lifting his chin as though straining to make out the sound.

“Listen.” Cynthia could hear muffled voices, the shuffle of feet, and the sound of metal scrapping the walls. She pushed him into the shadows and held her breath as the sounds stopped outside her door.

Constantine grabbed the sheath of his dagger and pulled her behind him. He placed his ear against the door. “All seems quiet,” he said after a time. “They have gone, my love.”

She pulled away. “You must go. It is not safe.”

“For you either.” His hand came up and the tips of his fingers touched her cheek.

“Safer than if Simon finds you in my chamber.”

Chapter Nine

Cynthia stood on the balcony of the inner bailey near the bower of her living quarters in the castle keep. The early morning breeze caught her hair, sending a golden strand across her cheek. She brushed it away, her blue eyes intently following Constantine as he quickly crossed the fixed bridge to the barbican and then disappeared through one of the openings normally used by archers near the rear gatehouse in the castle's outer curtain wall.

The sun had just appeared over the tree tops of the dense forest beyond and she shielded her eyes with her hand against its morning rays, straining through the brightness until she saw Constantine reach the edge of the glade. A brief turn back toward the castle, and then he disappeared into the thicket, their secret safe.

Her smile quickly faded when she caught sight of Simon entering the courtyard below. He fell to one knee and she watched him survey the footprints left in the moist ground. With a momentary look in her direction, he erased the tracks with an angry swipe of his hand before turning and striding away toward the heavy wooden door that led to the anteroom.

Quickly, Cynthia ran to her chamber, hoping to throw the bolt on her door chamber before Simon could reach her. She did not succeed.

"I did not give permission for a caller. Who was here?" he demanded, exploding into her room.

"No one, Sire" she assured him, hoping her voice did not betray her.

He grabbed her upper arm. "You lie. The footprints in the courtyard are fresh ones."

"No, my Lord. I swear. No one. Perhaps the footprints remained from the merchants."

"The hoof prints of the horses of my soldiers returning from patrol would have obliterated the footprints of the merchants," he quickly returned. He furrowed his brow, his eyes darkening to the color of thunderclouds. "Rather I think the footsteps left of a minstrel returning to finish his ballad."

Cynthia jerked her arm away. "And if it is?"

Simon gasped the hilt of the sword in its scabbard by his side, but did not unsheathe it. "He will not return if he values his throat."

"You would kill an unarmed man?" she challenged.

"I will kill a thief who tries to take my property."

Her eyes flared with the spark of kindled anger in reaction to his words. "I am no man's property, least of all yours!" Simon tried again to take hold of her arm, but she twisted away from him. "Do not touch me again." The tone in her voice underscored her warning.

He laughed in response and lunged for her. She moved quickly to her sleeping platform and pulled a dagger from beneath the bedding.

"I said, do not touch me. Taking over this castle and the lands around it does not mean you also take possession of me."

"Your father is dead and the man to whom you are promised shows no interest. The castle and everything in it belongs to me now," Simon reminded her in an emotionless voice. "And if anyone thinks he can take what is mine, he will hang like the common thief he is."

His words filled her with dread, but she dared not risk a show of weakness. Banishing the feeling to the place in her heart meant for memories, she squared her shoulders and took a step closer to him. "I belong to no one!" she shouted, the fire in her tone more than matching the heat of anger that now rose inside her chest. "And I remind you, the money you took from William's treasury is more than enough to pay for my care."

"The money will not last much longer. Soon you will have to earn your keep." Simon's gaze slid over her. "One way or another."

"Leave me now," she demanded, extending her arm and moving the dagger closer to him. "If you value your throat."

The muscle along his jaw tensed as his gaze shifted to the polished steel inches from his neck. "As you wish," he growled. At the door to her chamber, he paused. "But know when the time comes, I will take great pleasure in the fire in your belly." His gaze settled on her hips. "And the heat between your legs."

As the door to her chamber closed, Cynthia's body gave into to the tension. She shook so hard that the knife tumbled from her hand and hit the floor with a metallic clang. She ran to the chamber window.

"Be wary, Constantine, my love" she whispered to the wind, hoping it would take her words to him. "He knows."

****

Two men he could defeat. Maybe three. But from his hiding place behind a tangle of low bushes on the edge of the forest, Constantine counted five men in the glade between him and the castle. Guards. Lord Simon was suspicious.

He looked toward the west. The sun had begun its descent. As soon as the darkness engulfed the pastel-painted sky, Cynthia would come to the balcony and wait for him. Only a fool would defy the guards, he warned himself, drawing his fingers away from the grip of his sheathed sword. Or a man in love.

And Constantine was no fool.

He located his horse hidden among the trees a half-mile from the glade and led the animal back to the road. But before he could mount, a noise in the bushes stopped him. He spun around just in time to see a plain-clothed woman run toward him.

"Please, sir, I must speak to you."

He looked over his shoulder, hoping the soldiers were not searching the woods, and then back. "You are Cynthia's handmaiden. The one who brought the ointment to the monastery with the friar."

She nodded. "I am Jane."

"What are you doing the woods after dark?" he asked, keeping his voice low.

"I am charged to warn you," Jane said, "that Lord Simon sets a trap for you and you must not come to Cynthia this night."

Constantine's horse shuffled beside him, reminding him of the danger and he turned to calm it. When he turned back, Jane was gone. He started to call out to her, but heard the voices of the guards in the distance.

Swinging his leg up, he mounted the horse in one fluid motion. Then turning toward the town, he rode hard. He would heed the warning, but he would find away to see his beloved Cynthia.

****

The room above the inn was warm and scented by lamps burning sweet oil near the bed positioned in the center of the wall opposite the fire burning in the hearth. Light from the flames flickered and danced across the platform as though inviting a weary traveler to rest.

But Constantine lay on the cold, stone floor, head on a bedroll, arms folded across his chest. Serving the king had toughened him. Sometimes he fought for months on end to preserve the charge given to the Knights by King Arthur. Right must be defended against might and distress must be protected. Because of it he had no need for the feel of the soft straw covering the platform or for the unbleached linen pillows waiting for his head. The need he felt ran deep and only the touch of his lady's hand would still his eager heart.

But that would not be. Not tonight. Not ever if Lord Simon remained at Leyborne Castle.

Rising to sit, he rested a forearm on a bent knee and reached for a cup of wine from the decanter he set nearby. He drank deeply, thoughts of Cynthia nomadic in his mind. He tore his gaze from the embers of the fire. He had fought Turks,

Highlanders, Saxons, highwaymen and thieves, but he could not fight against the emptiness in his heart when she was not with him.

He removed his blue tunic and felt the cold metal of the emblem of the Knights of the Round Table fall against his skin. With his free hand, he angled it to his eyes. Given to him by King Arthur as part of the ceremony of his being a knight, the red dragon holding a cross meant to remind him of the Order's dominant idea; the love of a power greater than themselves, the love of men and noble deeds. To that he could now add, the love of a woman to which the love was returned ten fold.

He let the amulet fall back onto his chest and looked at the heavy wooden door of his room. In the stillness of the night he could hear the clatter of people in the tavern below. He yearned for the peace of sleep, the heaviness of nothingness, if only for a brief time, so he could escape into dreams of Cynthia's warm embrace. But he knew the night would be long and sleep would not come easily.

The scrape of the door latch opening made him turn fully toward the sound. He watched a cloaked and hooded figure enter and carefully close the door before sliding the bolt back into place. The figure turned and slowly lowered the dark hood that shrouded identity.

Constantine bolted to standing, the tunic he just removed falling from his hand. Cynthia. His dream had taken form.

He rose from his make-shift bed and crossed the room in three strides. As though trying to capture a dream, he took her into his arms. When his gaze locked with hers, he saw that her eyes burned red with tears.

"You risk too much to be here, milady," he said, his tone low and husky, his eyes roaming her face, branding it into his heart and memory.

"I could not bear to think I might never see you again," she whispered against his lips. His hair fell across her cheeks and mingled with her tears. "Lord Simon locked me in my room, posting guards outside the door. But Jane brought them wine laced with nightshade. They will sleep at their posts and remember nothing in the morning."

Constantine trailed a hand down her cheek before running his thumb across her lips. "I owe the lady a debt I will not forget."

Cynthia covered his hand with hers before kissing his palm. "As do I."

He looked down at her lovely face. "Lord Simon trusts no one. He will not rely on just the guards to keep you prisoner. You must return to the castle, before Simon discovers you are gone. I will come for you. I swear."

She shook her head, new tears forming. "But guards block the way. How can I believe this vow?"

"Have faith." He took her hand and pressed it to his bare chest. "Feel my heartbeat and know it beats only for you."

She looked into his eyes. His soft words reassured her, but she felt such heaviness in her heart. Suddenly needing to reaffirm their love in the face of her fear, she ran both hands up his chest, splaying her fingers across the breadth of the embossed muscles she found there. She felt his shudder and heard his breath catch as her fingertips caressed his neck before tracing his lips.

"Let me stay with you this night, Constantine," she pleaded, cupping his face before running her hands through the waves of his hair. The strands felt like silk moving across her skin as she continued. "Let us have perhaps this last night together before I return to my prison." Her voice caught. "Hold me in your arms so I can remember the feel of your body against mine when we are apart." She stepped out of his embrace, undid the fastenings of her cloak and let it fall from her shoulders. "If this be our last time together, let me be able to remember our love."

She wore nothing but a thin nightgown that did nothing to hide the curves and lines of her body. Light from the candles painted her in shades of gold. Awestruck by the vision she made, Constantine's desire threatened to break free. "Think well on this, Cynthia, for I know if I touch you this night, nothing will be able to stop me from showing you my love."

Cynthia stepped closer and wound her arms around his neck. His rock-hard body mirrored the need etched on his face, a need she had never seen on a man before. When he grabbed her bottom and pulled her snugly to him, she could feel the ridge of his sex press against her. Her breath caught at the contact.

"Is this what you want, Cynthia?" he whispered against her ear.

She took his hand and placed it on her breast. "Aye," she said.

Before she had time to think, his mouth slammed down on hers. Urgency came with his kiss.

His tongue prodded her mouth open and he plunged inside. Lightning shot through her as their tongues danced, igniting a passion in her long suppressed. She dug her fingers into his shoulders and struggled for balance, finding his skin surprisingly soft to her touch yet feeling his muscles harden and flex.

His arms snaked around her waist, hugging her close even as he kissed her. A second more and she nearly melted in his arms to become one with him as he lifted her effortlessly. Two strides and he placed her on the bed.

He stood over her, his eyes never leaving hers as he stripped off his pants and tossed hem aside. She glanced at the thick length of his manhood and felt her skin heat. It rose hard and high against his stomach from a thick patch of brown curls.

"Cynthia, come to your knees," she heard him say.

Not knowing why, she complied.

He grasped the hem of her garment and slid it up over her head. A slow smile spread over his face as he took in the sight of her wide-eyed and naked. Gently he pushed her back down onto the feather mattress and lowered himself on top of her.

Cynthia felt a moment of panic as his mouth found her breasts. It left as quickly as it came when his tongue circle her nipple with hot, lazy strokes. Part of her marked every stroke of his tongue, while part of her wondered what he would do next. Never before had she imagined that a man's touch could arouse such a need within her.

With a jolt, she arched her back as he began to suck hard on her nipple until it pebbled into a hot, aching bud. In turn he did one, then the other until she bit on her lower lip to stifle a groan.

His hand moved to her stomach and she tensed. “Trust me, my love,” Constantine whispered, pressing a kiss against her stomach. “It will be sweet.”

When he spread her legs cool air teased her flesh. She felt exposed and forced herself to relax, but she was unprepared for what he did next. His finger slid into her and she bucked.

“No, sweet, I need to prepare you,” he said. “I wish to make the first time as pleasant as I can.”

His fingers probed her over and over, his mouth returning to her tender nipples. Sensations soared and tremors raced through her until she cried out. In and out his fingers played until she moistened, telling him that her body lay ready for him.

He stopped his play and moved up her body, his hands braced alongside her. He dipped his head and kissed her lips, her cheeks, her forehead as he lowered himself onto her. His sex, hard and hot, pressed against her. He hesitated, just for a heartbeat, before taking her mouth fully with his and pushing inside her.

His kiss smothered her cry when he bucked his hips and entered her. Inside her now, he continued to kiss her even as he thrust forward, deeply, fully, stretching her for him. Then he held still.

Cynthia felt as though she would be torn apart, but then he began to move again and the sensations changed. Constantine thrust his manhood in and out of her and soon her body seemed no longer under her control. She began to match his movements. She grasped his buttock and arched upward to take every inch of him that she could.

She writhed and sobbed and rocked with the rapture she felt. Intense pleasure, almost too much for her to bear, made her cry out his name. "Constantine!"

"My love. Am I hurting you?" he asked.

"Only a little, but I do not want you to stop." Her body glistened with the sheen of love. "These feelings, I do not know what I am to do."

"We are joining, my sweet. Trust what they tell you to do."

He continued moving, driving, retreating pushing in and out until she could hardly stand it. Pressure built until she finally screamed in the ultimate pleasure. Her muscles contracted, and heat, like molten lava, flooded her. Constantine pumped harder, crying out her name as he emptied inside her. The sound of their labored breathing filled the room.

Arms entwined, they lay together as one, even their hair tangling in its own mating ritual. Cynthia smiled and pushed Constantine's wayward locks away from his face. "I have oft wondered what it would be like to lay with a man. But nothing I could have ever imagined could rival this." She bit down on her lower lip. "I know you have lain with other women. Did I disappoint?"

He kissed her shoulder before looking into her eyes. "I will never lay with another," he promised. "What we have just experienced is more than the primal need of man for woman, it is most precious. I need only to remember this moment," he whispered, "and I will be in heaven."

She lifted her head. His dark lashes veiled the sensual fire in his eyes. He smiled and stretched like a sleepy cat content in warmth of the sun. She ran her fingertips across his lips and kissed his shoulder.

"I am yours forever," Cynthia murmured.

"And I am yours," he agreed.

She took his lips with hers. Her hands began to explore his body, even as she rubbed herself against him.

He arched a dark eyebrow. "My lady, the day grows near." His mouth curved in a mischievous smile. "We should not begin something that would be hurried." He ran a single finger down her neck and across her breast, feeling her tremble at his touch. "And if I'm not mistaken, you must prepare to mourn for your betrothed."

Cynthia tensed with his words. "I was a child when my father announced the betrothal, and Sir William nearly twenty years my senior. They went away to join Arthur and I moved into Leyborne Castle to await their return. Then I had no choice. I became resigned that I would have to bend to the will of a man I did not know, marry someone not of my own choosing, and bear a child simply for a man's pride." She closed her eyes. "When I grieve for his death, I will not mourn being released from my fate. If that makes me wicked, then I am guilty of the sin."

"Angels do not sin," Constantine reminded her, his finger tracing small circles on her stomach.

"If not sins, then perhaps even angels have wants."

He brushed a lock of golden hair from her cheek. "And what does my angel want?" he asked as he ran his fingertips down the curve of her face before tracing her mouth.

She felt her breath catch with his caress. “I wish to marry a man I love, at a time of mutual choice and have his child from mutual desire.”

“All that and more you will do,” Constantine promised.

Cynthia’s heartbeat rose with anticipation. “Will you court me as though one would a lover?”

He did not hesitate in his response. “I would.”

She smiled, concealing the pang of guilt her question aroused in her. Why had she asked him that? Having no dowry, she could offer him nothing. She had no right to ask him to defy Lord Simon and accept only her love in return. She sat up, gathered her gown and her cloak and brushed the tangles from her hair with her fingertips.

Constantine rose with her and looked at her with drawn brows. “Have I made you feel uneasy, milady?” he asked, watching as she dressed and then draped the cloak over her shoulders.

“No,” she reassured, casting a glance over her shoulder at the lightening sky. “But the sunrise disturbs me well enough. I must return to the castle.”

Constantine looked at the rays of light spreading up in the eastern horizon. “I’ll take you as close to the castle as I dare by horse. We must go quickly. We are already taking more chances than we should.”

****

Cynthia walked lightly between the sleeping guards outside her chamber. As she pushed open the door, one of them rustled coming close to awareness. She paused, daring not to even breathe.

As he settled back in sleep, a hand reached to her from inside the room. "Quickly, they will wake soon."

Cynthia glanced down at the soldiers as she entered her chamber. "I was not missed?"

As quietly as possible, Jane closed the heavy wooden door. "Using the back stairs, Lord Simon came to see you once during the evening. But the bed curtains were drawn and I blocked his way, saying you fell ill with a malady of the stomach and were sleeping. He had been drinking and that made it easy to lead him away. But I suspect that once the consequences of too much wine have worn off, he will return."

A wave of relief for the time given her washed over Cynthia as she took Jane's hand. "I owe you much," she said. "If I had means, I would free you from your service here so you could follow the in the way of your mother."

Jane took the cloak from Cynthia's shoulders. Carefully folding the dark fabric, she laid it over a small bench near the wall. "Not yet, my lady. I have much yet to do before I take my freedom."

"Maybe soon we can also be free of Lord Simon," Cynthia mused.

"Perhaps," Jane agreed, unlacing Cynthia's dress and waiting until she slipped it from her body. Taking it, Jane folded it into the trunk at the foot of the bed and watched as Cynthia donned a clean white muslin sleep dress before slipping into bed. A smile grew on Jane's face when she arranged the coverlet. "I think the perfume of love clings to your skin," she said.

Cynthia stretched like a contented cat. "Aye, it does," she replied, smiling, "a scent more beautiful than all the flowers in the garden."

Jane reached for the vial of rosewater on the table next to the bed. "I don't think Lord Simon would agree."

Chapter Ten

Cynthia awoke as the bright light of midday crossed her face. She rose from the bed, the stone floor cold on her feet as she reached for her robe.

She looked over. Jane's bed was empty. She had put out a new dress the color of field lavender with a leather belt, on a stool near the fireplace, along with a pair of new sandals. Cynthia dressed and walked to the window.

In the courtyard below where colonnade framed a small garden, she could see Jane gathering flowers into a basket. No one but she and Jane knew the secrets that also hid among the blooms.

In silence, Jane practiced the old ways, keeping sacred the rituals and remedies passed down to her from her mother, a Druid Priestess. Cynthia was alive today because of the healing arts they practiced.

Shortly after Cynthia came to the castle, she developed a raging fever from a cut to her leg. The court physician had given up hope and called for the bishop to hear Cynthia's last confession. That night Jane brewed a strong tea from among herbs she had hidden among her meager possessions. During the night Cynthia's fever broke and by daybreak, her breathing eased. The physician and the bishop declared it a miracle of God, but Cynthia and Jane knew otherwise.

Since Lord Simon had taken over the shire, he openly hunted those who still held to the goddess. After capture he sent them to Mordred who decided their providence. Though he suspected that Jane held to the earth-mother traditions, he had not acted on his suspicions. Yet.

How long Jane would be spared, Cynthia could not know. But she did know she would protect Jane at all costs. She would not allow Simon to prove Jane practiced the arts and send her to Mordred no matter what the cost might be. She closed her eyes, pain tearing at her heart. She may have to offer her body to the man she loathed in order to protect those she loved. She could only continue to pray that Arthur's knights came quickly.

She heard the wooden doors to her chamber open and turned to the sound. Looming like and immovable boulder, Simon stood in the doorway, his silhouette darkly outlined by the light from the hallway.

"Lady Cynthia," he said, slowly walking toward her, "I trust you slept well?"

She swallowed hard but held her ground as he approached. "Well enough."

"Jane said you fell ill." He stepped to her and circled her like a vulture sensing prey.

"A slight bout with a malady of the stomach."

"Passed?" he asked.

"The difficulty left me by dawn."

He took a lock of blond hair and rolled it between his fingers before bringing the strand to his face. He inhaled. "Roses," he said. "As sweet as roses." His eyes never left Cynthia's as he dropped the strand from his fingers in an exaggerated gesture.

"Jane drew some water so I could bathe, and scented it." She stepped away from his reach. "It did refresh me."

Simon clapped his hands together. "Good. Then you will be fit enough to join me. I have planned a Summer Feast to celebrate May Day." He turned and began to leave before spinning back on his heels to face Cynthia. "Oh, and I have sent for the minstrel. I know how much you enjoy his song." His gaze held hers, obviously waiting for her to react.

Though icy fingers of foreboding wound themselves around her heart, she did not give him the satisfaction.

****

A herald's trumpet marked the official beginning of the Summer Feast. Villagers already filled the castle courtyards from outside the wall. Now they mingled with the performers and the jugglers, partaking eagerly of the heaping platters of food and freely flowing ale being passed around for them.

Lady Cynthia waited in the great hall with Jane by her side as the official procession entered through the massive, ironbound doors. Lord Simon led the assemblage, his soldiers at his side. The invited guests watched as they filed behind the massive wooden table set in the center of the hall.

"Let the feast begin," Simon commanded, sitting and emptying his jewel-encrusted goblet of its wine as the guests cheered.

At once the hall exploded into activity. Pages brought exotic meats from the kitchen, steam rising from them in fragrant clouds. A servant, struggling under the weight of a large platter, deposited a large bird in the center of the head table.

"A peacock," one of the Lords exclaimed, leaning forward to examine the dish. "Lord Simon spared no expense today, as these creatures only roam well beyond the sea."

Cynthia reluctantly took her place at Simon's right, wondering how she would be able to eat anything. Intuition prickled at her. Constantine was here. With soldiers posted at every exit, she feared for his safety.

Through a trusted courier, she sent a message to Constantine, begging him not to accept Simon's invitation, saying she would rather bear an evening without him than have him in harm's way. But he refused to be kept from her, his returning note saying that just to see her would be worth any risk.

"So, my dear," Simon began, dabbing at his chin with the edge of his silken sleeve. "You are enjoying the festivities?"

She smiled, grateful the activity in the hall had distracted him until now. "Well enough, Sire."

Simon reached across and patted her hand. "I know your desire." Clapping his hand together, he signaled to a guard at the door. "Send in the minstrel for my Lady."

Cynthia smothered the gasp that rose in her throat. Standing in the entrance, framed by the massive metal-bound portals, stood her beloved, Constantine. He entered followed by musicians.

As he walked toward the head table, she hoped Simon would not notice how Constantine's eyes held hers, or how quickly her rapidly beating heart spread a warm flush across her cheeks.

"Minstrel," Lord Simon said in a booming voice when Constantine reached the head table. "A song." He took Cynthia by the arm and pulled her to standing. "To the Lady Cynthia." Simon raised his right hand to the crowd. "A love song." The attendees shouted their approval as Simon hauled Cynthia around the table and deposited her directly in front of Constantine. There his gaze narrowed. "Sing as though you were her lover," he commanded.

Cynthia lowered her eyes, willing her body not to tremble. Lusty shouts filled the hall. "My Lord," she lifted her chin to meet Simon's gaze. "Do not give the man such an impossible task."

Before Simon could comment, Constantine took her hand and led her to a nearby bench. "Milady, for someone as beautiful as you, the task will be a pleasure."

She sat and Constantine quieted the crowd with a wave of his hand. He turned to Simon and bowed, before once again taking Cynthia's hand. He touched it to his lips, his tongue snaking out, swirling on her skin in a secret sensual greeting meant only for her. "Do not fear, my love," he whispered, falling to one knee. "It will be a love song indeed."

Cynthia nearly forgot to breathe as Constantine began. His voice vibrated through her, its mellow tones touching every fiber of her being, bringing her body to a fine-tuned awareness only of him. He sang of the joy of man and woman and the love that could grow from first kiss. Through the lyrics, she thought only of him and the night they shared.

His words touched her, reminding her how his hands explored her body and her soul with such tenderness and skill that she knew there could never be another for her. She looked into his eyes and she knew by the fire she saw there that he felt the same. In the final words of the song he sang, he thanked God for sending an angel to earth.

As the last trill of the lute strings faded, their eyes held for what seemed to be an eternity. Her heart beat faster and she longed to take him in her arms. Just as she was ready to act upon her need, Simon stepped between them. Cynthia's gazed lifted to see his dark eyes flash with animosity of such intenseness that she feared for her own life.

Thinking only of Constantine's safety, she snatched a goblet from the tray of a passing servant. She held it high. "To Lord Simon! And the children the minstrel's song will help conceive this night!"

Bawdy cheers answered her toast. As the revelers began to press closer to their host, Cynthia dropped the goblet and grabbed Constantine's hand. Together they ran through the crowd and fled from the hall.

Chapter Eleven

Hand in hand Cynthia and Constantine climbed the stairs to her room. Once inside Cynthia slid the bolt into place. “We can rest here for only a moment. The gaiety will not distract Simon for long. He will notice we both are gone.”

“I will not put you in danger,” Constantine said.

“I will choose my own path,” she assured. “My time under the authority of Lord Simon is nearly at an end and he knows this. I will work the fields or spin cloth if I must, but I will be free of him.”

He looked at her pale blond hair swirling around her shoulders and cascading down her back. The way her delicate lips glistened in the light from the torches on the wall nearly unraveled his will. He said nothing, but traversed the room to the crossed swords that hung on the wall opposite her bed. He reached up and wrapped his fingers around the hilt of one of them and yanked it free. “You will be rid of him,” he promised.

Cynthia’s eyes widened. “You’d make a stand for me? Here?”

“If it be the will of the Almighty.”

She stepped behind him, leaning over his right shoulder with one hand on his arm to share his view of the extraordinary weapon in his hand. Gems of purple, red and green crusted the golden hilt. The polished silver blade flashed a brilliance that could mesmerize.

"William gave my father this room when we moved into the castle. After they left for Camelot, I moved my things here needing to still feel close to father. I only always thought of the swords as decoration," she said, tracing his knuckles with her fingers, "but in your hand, this one is magnificent." She let her hand drift up his arm to his shoulders, feeling him tense as she did.

"'Tis a fine weapon," Constantine agreed. He raised the blade in a defending motion.

When he moved, Cynthia could feel his muscles harden and smell the faint aroma of soap blend with the warmth rising on his skin. She lowered her hand and stepped back. The last thing she needed was to feel his solid body beneath her palm. With the prospect of Simon finding them at any moment, she could not allow a fleeting moment of desire to distract her, no matter how much she loved the distraction.

Purposely ignoring the way his hair curled behind his ears, she focused on the sword in his hand. "The markings at the end," she said, seeing a dragon, a crown, a cup and an arrow among the many symbols etched in the metal. "What do they mean?"

"They are ancestral markings, etched in the metal by those who have used the blade in battle." Constantine grasped the sword at the top of the hilt with his right hand and pointed with his left to an area just below his palm. "There. See it? The Cross. The sword maker stamped the markings precisely at the right point to rest in the palm of the hand. Many warriors believe that resting the cross in one's hand during battle will bring protection from the Saints."

He took a step back and swung the sword in front of him in a wide arc. "It's the prefect weight and size for the fight. The craftsmanship is exquisite." He took another step back and then pivoted, slicing through the air with power and grace.

He let the sword drop to his side, but kept his hand firmly on the grip. His eyes glistened. "And I will use it to protect you now with my life, if necessary."

She raised an eyebrow. "You'd kill for me?"

"If I must." He kept the ancient weapon in his hand, twirling it at his side as if it had been made just for him.

Cynthia looked at the tapestry that hung above her bed. "You look like him." The knight woven there had shoulder length dark hair that curled out from beneath a silver helmet. Clad in full armor and mounted on a horse, he held his sword high, fighting a contingent of Saxon barbarians holding spears and swords. Behind him, a woman with hair the color of sunlight waited in a gray tower for rescue.

"Perhaps the tapestry holds a prophecy as well," he said.

She waved off the thought. The knight in the picture was covered in blood. She did not want to speculate whether or not the weaver intended for it to be his or that of the enemy he fought. "No. It's just a picture."

Constantine twisted the sword in his hand, just as the rear door to Cynthia's bedchamber crashed open. A group of guards surrounded them. The circle they made opened only briefly to allow Simon and another man to enter it before it closed around them once again. Constantine raised the sword and pulled Cynthia close.

"I believe you know Ranulf, the stone carver," Simon said.

Constantine eyed the man. "We've met."

Simon pointed to Constantine. "Is that the man you saw, stone carver?"

"Aye, my Liege," Ranulf said, "I saw him with the lady in the woods. He put her on his horse and rode away."

"And did the lady go willingly?" Simon asked.

"She was crying. Sobbin' like one without hope."

"My Lord," Cynthia said, trying to pull away from Constantine, "I…"

Constantine tugged her back to him. "Say nothing," he warned in a whisper only she could hear as Simon's men stepped closer in response. "I fear this is a staged maneuver."

"Anything else?" Simon asked Ranulf.

Ranulf looked from Simon's face to Constantine's. "No," he replied, holding Constantine's gaze. "Nothing."

Simon tossed Ranulf a velvet pouch. "Leave us," he ordered.

Ranulf bounced the purse up and down in his hand a few times before bowing to his lord and leaving.

Simon turned slowly back, his face twisted into a scowl, the thin beard he wore emphasizing the cruel line of his mouth. "You stand accused of kidnapping," he said to Constantine, clearly fighting to keep his anger in check. "What say you?"

Constantine did not reply, but instead caressed Cynthia's back in a consoling gesture made to reassure. When she looked at him, he saw anger build in her eyes, and he attempted to quell it with a slight shake of his head.

"Nothing? You have no defense?"

Constantine knew Simon would not attack first, preferring to wait for him to react. He would not.

"And now you break into a lady's bed chamber," Simon's gaze fell to the sword in Constantine's hand, "armed, no less." Extending his arms, Simon paced the ring surrounding them, addressing his guards. "Let all men present bear witness that this minstrel entered Lady Cynthia's room, intent on using a weapon to force her to submit to him." On a signal from Simon, a burly guard grasped Cynthia by the shoulders and pulled her away from Constantine.

"He did none of that," Cynthia countered, surging against the hands that held her fast.

Ignoring her, Simon continued, the curl of his lip accentuating the anger clearly etched on his face. "I challenge the accused now, to a fight of honor so I may save the lady's reputation. Unless…" he paused, eyes alive with menace. He took a step closer to Constantine. "Unless, of course, cowardice stops you."

Constantine responded to the insult by raising the sword and adopting a fighting stance. He nodded his intent to accept.

"I see the minstrel thinks he can use a sword," Simon further taunted.

"Find out just how much," Constantine challenged.

"No," Cynthia cried. She angled her body to Constantine as much as her captor would allow it. "He baits you. Simon is a skilled swordsman."

The two men circled each other in the slow search for an opening, Simon holding his blade low in an invitation for Constantine to strike first. Complying with the challenge, Constantine raised his sword and thrust it forward. In a clang of steel upon steel the combat began.

Cynthia watched in horror as swift parries kept both men off balance. After what felt like an eternity with neither man gaining the advantage and with a quick series of strikes and counters, Simon's blade whipped out. The tip sliced upward through Constantine's shirt, splitting fabric and leather, forcing him to step backward to try to avoid its sting, but a thin dark red line formed across his cheek. Constantine's hand went up to his face and came away with blood.

Cynthia felt her body grow as cold as ice when Simon broke into mocking laughter before pulling a small knife that had been tucked inside his belt. "Constantine," she cried out, "a dagger."

Simon sprang forward, aiming the knife in his hand for Constantine's chest. But Constantine sidestepped the attack and pushed Simon squarely in the back making him stumble. With renewed fervor, Constantine pressed forward, his sword cutting wide arcs back and forth in an attack. Simon barely dodged the blows as they drove him backward.

Regaining his balance, Simon planted his feet wide and lunged forward hoping to catch Constantine in mid-swing. But Constantine spun in a tight circle and brought his blade across Simon's left arm. Cursing as a stain of red spread across the sleeve of his shirt, Simon staggered to the side.

Constantine lowered his sword. "The fight is done. Just let us go."

Simon appeared to comply just long enough to see Constantine relax his vigilance. Then twisting his wrist in an upward motion, he smashed the hilt of his sword against Constantine's temple.

Senses weakened by the force of the blow, Constantine's hand opened, releasing the sword. He fell to his knees, struggling against unconsciousness with Cynthia's screams echoing in his brain. He was only marginally aware of Simon approaching him before his side exploded with pain. The last thing he saw before the blackness overtook him was the blade of a dagger in Simon's hand covered in blood.

Chapter Twelve

Cynthia knelt on the floor where the unconscious body of her love lie before the guards dragged him away. The doors to her bedchamber were bolted from the outside and two guards stood watch on her balcony. Though she pounded on the heavy wooden doors until her hands were raw and bleeding, no one answered her cries.

Constantine may very well be dead by now. She had no way of knowing what happened to him after the guards dragged him from the room, and could do no more than wait.

She dipped a rag in the bucket of water at her side and wiped his blood from the timber floor. Out of the corner of her eye, a glint of gold glistened from underneath her wooden clothes chest.

She crept toward it, rapt by the gleam. Sweeping her hand along the floor beneath the chest, she closed her fingers around a circular object. When she brought it out, she gasped. She held the amulet Constantine wore around his neck. Rising to sitting, she examined the leather strap holding it, and discovered it had been cut during the fight.

Pressing it to her chest, she said a silent prayer of thanksgiving to the Almighty for not allowing Simon to find it. If Simon knew a Knight of Camelot had been beneath his blade, he would have surely ended Constantine's life right then.

She removed the charm from its leather cord and slipped it into the bodice of her gown. There, resting near her heart, it would be safe.

After finishing her sorrowful task, she put the bucket next to the fireplace and looked around the room. The fire burned in its last fading ember, the room dark except for a moonbeam of light filtering in through the window. She spent the last few hours waiting and praying for Constantine. Despite her pleas, Simon refused to tell her what he planned for her love, the bitter ache in her heart inflamed by each passing hour.

Unable to sleep, she paced the room, waiting. As she passed the chamber door, it swung open, framing Simon and several men in light coming from torches in the hall. Even as a cry formed on her lips, a large hand covered her mouth. Terror gripped her as her assailant caught both her wrists in his free hand with a strength that defied her imagination.

"I've come to claim the spoils of combat," he said, triumph in his tone.

"Where is Constantine? What have you done with him?" she asked in a rush of breath when he took his hand from her mouth. She struggled as he pulled her closer to him, trying vainly to free her hands. She kicked out. "I need to tend to his wound."

"No need to waste time on him. He'll be dead soon enough."

"He's alive?" Cynthia felt hope race in her heart.

"He still breathes for the moment."

"Thank the Lord." Buoyed by the knowledge that her beloved still lived, Cynthia struggled harder to free herself. In the tussle a small table near the door overturned, sending the books atop it crashing to the floor with a thud.

"Enough of that," Simon spat, circling her wrists with rope and thrusting a cloth into her mouth to gag her. "We must not wake the servants." Seizing her by the waist, he lifted her easily onto his shoulder.

Simon strode into the hall, his squirming bundle an easy weight on his shoulders. There several of his most trusted guards waited, swords drawn.

"Come," Simon said to them, "I have what I need here. We ride for Donahyde Castle to gather the army."

****

Jane barely exited the staircase leading to Cynthia's solar when she heard the sound of a scuffle coming from the end of the dimly lit hallway. Her first thought was to race toward it, but Simon's voice made her retreat into the shadows. Her heartbeat quickened as the contingent of soldiers moved passed her. She heard Cynthia's muffled screams and saw her perched on Simon's shoulder, guards surrounding them.

Reaching into the pocket of her gown, Jane grasped the hilt of the small dagger she kept there. Ready to fight for her lady's life, she surged forward when a hand grabbed her from behind.

"Not now, Jane," a voice warned. "It would be at the cost of your life and then Lady Cynthia would truly be alone." The last soldier in line pushed her back into the shadows. "I'll do what I can for her. You must help the minstrel. Simon threw him half-dead into in the dungeons."

Jane nodded and watched him leave thanking the Almighty that all soldiers did not follow Lord Simon.

****

"You're late," the jailer barked as he unlocked the iron grated-door leading to the prison cells beneath the castle. Behind it, a woman with a large bucket waited. "Maybe the vermin in the cells can miss their dinner, but there's hell to pay if I miss mine." He watched the her enter, her face shadowed in the dim torchlight by the hood of a cloak. "You're not Mary," he said as she passed him. He grabbed her backside with his large hand and squeezed. "Too scrawny." He dipped his head, straining to get a better look at her face.

Jane prayed the jailer wouldn't recognize her and pulled her cloak tighter around her with her free hand. "Mary's sick. The cook just told me to bring this here." She set down the iron pot on the ground and stirred the contents with the coarse wooden ladle set inside, the aroma of gravy and meat rising.

The jailer grabbed a wooden bowl from among his things in a dingy pack on the floor. "A healthy scoop, woman," he ordered, holding it out to her.

After setting the large iron pot on the table next to the door, Jane loaded the ladle with stew. Her hand shook as she dished it into the soldier's bowl, a cut of meat falling to the dirt floor.

"No use letting that go to waste," the jailer said, picking it up with dirty, fleshy fingers and dropping it back into the pot. "They won't care."

By now the prisoners who could still move stuck filthy bowls out from between the irons bars of their cells. One by one Jane put a measure of brown potage into each one. As soon as the food filled the bowl, the captive would retreat to the far side of his cell.

"Don't waste food on that one," the jailer called out when she approached the last cell. "If that one doesn't die by morning, he's scheduled to be executed."

Jane lowered the ladle and started back to the door. She hadn't gotten two steps when the jailer's eyes suddenly widened. He extended his hand as he took a shaky step toward her, his mouth open in a silent question. Before he could speak, he collapsed with a loud thud.

She held her breath and waited. Then satisfied the guard was unconscious, she set the ladle and pot down and approached the fallen man. Extending her foot, she nudged him with the tip of her shoe. He did not move. Again, she jabbed at him. He lay still.

With both hands she lowered her hood. Then, with an energy brought on from anger, she kicked the prone man in his stomach. "Don't ever touch a lady unless invited," she said between clenched teeth, her voice a whisper tinged with disgust. She kicked him again. "Especially one that cares only about the man in the last cell and knows how to season stew with nightshade."

The only reply came in a low groan.

Jane found the keys on the jailer's belt. Despite the prisoners also affected by the drugged stew, she opened each cell, whispering a prayer that a benevolent angel would help them escape before their jailer awoke. When she got to the last cell, she threw open the door and grabbed a torch from its place on the wall.

Stooping as she entered to avoid the low ceiling, she held the torch as high as she could and looked desperately around the dark, damp cell. She shuddered as fear closed her throat when she saw him.

Constantine lay on the dirt floor, his skin pale, and his breath so shallow that she felt compelled to bend and rest an ear on his chest to prove to herself that he still lived. An examination of his injury showed a deep stab wound, the cut already swollen and discolored. With a sinking feeling, she realized it was already ulcerating.

Rising, she took the torch to the small grated window near the ceiling and waved the light back and forth in front of it. Confident the signal would be observed, she carefully leaned it against the wall near Constantine.

"You will not die," she whispered to him. "I will not let you."

The words were barely out when three men swarmed around them. Jane directed them to carry Constantine out of the cell and out into the courtyard. She knew the effort might kill him, but also knew they needed to move quickly. The jailer would not sleep much longer.

Once outside, the men set Constantine on a makeshift litter built by lashing spears together. He groaned as they began to move him, a sign to Jane that he might still be helped.

"We'll take him to the cloister at the far end of the shire," she said, running along with them. "Most of it still stands intact and we can find shelter there."

As they spirited Constantine away, their movements produced unintentional jolts to his body. He groaned as the jarring caused his wound to bleed again. In response to the pain, he grasped violently at the air as though fighting an unseen foe.

Jane touched his shoulder and he seemed to calm. "Soon, good knight. Soon you will continue your fight with your enemy. But for now, your foe is the fever."

Chapter Thirteen

The dark spires on Donahyde Castle loomed in the distance. Built into a cliff at the foot of imposing mountains it had been raised from the ruins of a fortress built long ago by conquerors long forgotten. The bastion had withstood many sieges and judging by the daunting sight of it, Cynthia guessed it could endure one more.

Bound and gagged, she had been forced to make the trip riding with Simon, his arms wrapped around her. When his horse stopped, he forced her face upward so she could see the daunting structure the castle made as one saw it for the first time. "Welcome to your new home, my Lady. Mordred has been kind enough to prepare a room especially for you."

He laughed in response to the disgust on her face. Dismounting first, he pulled her into his arms and easily carried her into the fortress.

Inside the courtyard she could see men, armed and grim-faced, attending a variety of tasks. Some sharpened weapons while others piled supplies in wagons. It seemed to her as though they prepared for war.

Simon carried her down a long dark stairway to the dungeons, and, after entering a remote cell, dropped her unceremoniously into a pile of damp straw. Faint threads of light filtered in through holes in the ceiling and water droplets clung to the stones that made up the wall. The damp smell threatened to overcome her as Simon finally unbound her wrists and removed her gag.

"I know these accommodations are not as lavish as those you are used to." He bent low in a mocking bow. "But they are home."

"Why did you bring me here?" she demanded.

"The people of the sire love you," he explained. "They would not take kindly to the..." he stopped and lowered his gaze to Cynthia's breasts, "…the education I plan on giving you here. Once you understand what is expected of you, you will return as my wife."

As he lifted his gaze, Cynthia's anger flared and she spit into his face. "Then I will never see Leyborne Castle again for nothing you can do will ever cause me to accept you."

Simon dragged a hand down his cheek to remove the insult. "I know you think I'm a monster, but it matters not. Think on this," he leaned toward her. "Your father is dead, your betrothed has abandoned you and you have no lands, no wealth, no protector." His hand swept the cell as he spoke. "This is all you deserve." He took her chin in his hand and angled her face to his. "But if you do your part, you will not suffer."

Cynthia pulled free and shrank back against the wall. "Never. Constantine will release me from this torture."

Simon was beside her in two strides. He took her by the waist. "If your troubadour is not dead by now, he will be at dawn." He pulled her to him. "You will accept me, Cynthia, as you did him. And I demand not only your submission, but also your sincere desire."

She turned her head away as his lips descended toward hers. "I'd rather die here."

"That can be arranged." Simon stepped back from her. "Do not think for one moment that you cannot be made to suffer until you change your mind."

"I will never change my mind," she vowed.

Simon's face contorted with anger and his raised his hand. Cynthia did not shrink from the threat, but closed her eyes, squared her shoulders and waited for the blow.

None came.

She opened her eyes in time to see Simon leave the cell, slamming the door with a powerful clang. It's reverberation sounded to Cynthia like the crash of a crypt lid closing.

Running to the heavy door, she tried to find a handle. There was none. Cells like these were made to only open from the outside. She closed her eyes and prayed; not for herself but for Constantine. She prayed that Simon was wrong. Constantine could not be dead. She thought of his bravery and his strength and knew what she needed to do.

She would be strong, bold. For him. Until he came to save her.

****

The sun set slowly through the age-worn arches of the church where once stained glass bore pictures of the saints. Jane and her confederates laid Constantine as gently as possible on the crude bed Jane had prepared. But the movement produced an unintentional twist of his body and he gasped again in agony.

Jane touched his face and his eyelids fluttered open revealing pain-clouded eyes. With great difficulty he raised his hand and whispered Cynthia's name before his eyes closed and his hand dropped lifelessly.

He was hallucinating, Jane concluded. The pain must be great. She pressed a hand to his heart and found a weak but steady beat. Lifting her chin, she whispered a prayer to whatever saints still resided in the remains of the church and begged they intercede to keep him alive.

"Build a fire," she ordered the men who helped her spirit Constantine away. "We must keep him warm. And I need water to cleanse his wound." She unbound her medicine pouch from her belt.

Lifting his bloodied tunic, she found a deep stab wound where the blade of Simon's sword had slashed through him. The gash was swollen and discolored and she knew she would have to work quickly to save his life. She cleansed the area and packed the wound with the lady's mantle poultice she made from herbs she grew in the garden of Leyborne Caste. Satisfied she could do no more, she covered the wound with a cloth soaked in water containing comfrey to stop the bleeding.

As the warmth of a crackling fire grew, she brewed a strong tea made from yarrow and lemon to aid in healing. She would force Constantine to drink whenever pain brought him to the brink of consciousness.

"You will not die," she whispered into his ear, holding his head and bringing the wooden cup to his lips. "And you will be with Cynthia again."

****

In the damp foulness of the cell in the bowels of Donahyde Castle the days passed slowly, each its own nightmare. Weakened by the treatment she endured, a rattling cough rose from Cynthia's chest seeming to sap what little strength she had. The meager food Simon allowed her, she eagerly ate, clinging to the hope that Constantine still lived. After all, she reasoned, if he were indeed dead, there would be no reason for Simon to continue to keep her captive.

Still, Constantine had not come for her and she feared him mortally ill from the wound inflicted by Simon. Closing her eyes and lifting her chin, she prayed he would stay alive until she could get to him.

She renewed her vow to be strong. She would be clever, cunning. Duplicity would be her ally and she would prevail. She would live and somehow avenge the evil Simon had wrought across the land. And she would be again with Constantine.

Outside her prison, a thunderstorm rose. Rain drained into her cell in streams from cracks in the wall. She crawled, shivering, into a corner where a measure of dryness remained. There she rubbed her upper arms, attempting to return warmth to her skin.

Suddenly the door swung open and Simon stepped into the cell. Dragging her roughly to her feet by her wrists, he laughed. "How fares the fiery

Lady Cynthia today?" he asked in a voice tinged with rebuke.

Remembering her vow to survive, she went limp in his arms and sagged against him.

"This is most unexpected," he said, lifting her chin with his fingertips, "and most delightful."

He grasped the back of her head and pulled her face to his. He kissed her hard and it took everything inside her for her not to resist. When he stepped back, his eyes glowed with lust, and she shuddered at his obvious arousal.

"Though I did not expect you to see the uselessness of your struggles so soon, I am pleased to find you are as intelligent as you are beautiful." He wound his hand in her hair and pulled her back into his embrace.

Praying for the strength to bear what would come, Cynthia did not fight him as he kissed her mouth then her throat. She needed to think...and quick. If he touched her, he would find the amulet of Camelot that she had hidden near her heart.

She forced herself to lift her hand to his cheek. "My Lord," she whispered, "I am dirty, my clothes soiled. Surely you do not want this to be our first time together."

"It matters not to me," Simon's voice hoarse, his breath uneven with desire. He swept her up and placed her on a crude table just outside the cell.

"Please," Cynthia continued as Simon held her down and began to loosen his belt cord. "You deserve to be pleasured in comfort, lying on pelts, covered with fine cloth. Not among the rodents and insects."

"You've caused me much trouble, Lady," Simon's gruff voice growled into her ear. He pulled her dress up to her waist exposing her. His hand trailed up her thigh. "I will take my release here."

Cynthia struggled against his searching fingers. "Please, my Lord. I am your willing servant. It could be more for you, much more."

"I have waited long enough for you. I will wait no longer." His fingers squeezed her thigh as his mouth descended onto hers.

Cynthia forced her lips to be pliant against his though her stomach lurched and the taste of bile rose in her throat. "Take me to a proper bed," she said against his lips. "And I will please you beyond your wildest dreams." She ran her tongue against his and forced her body to settle under his hand.

The groping stopped. Simon raised his head, drawing in a ragged breath. "Swear it," his gaze fell to his hand, poised between her thighs to claim her.

"It will be nothing like you have known, I swear it," Cynthia promised. Her stomach lurched again as she felt his fingers graze her mound when he stepped away from her.

Turning away, he opened the outer door to the line of prison cells and called out, "Prepare this woman for travel. Tell Mordred we return to Leyborne Castle in one hour."

Turning to Cynthia, he grabbed her throat with a powerful hand and squeezed until he heard her gasp for air. "I warn you this better not be a trick.

Chapter Fourteen

Jane kept her vigil over Constantine, fearing that each moment might be his last. Fever besieged him, and she cooled him with cloths soaked with water. Again and again she forced him to drink the potion she prepared fresh each day, but as the fever raged, his strength waned. Angry streaks of scarlet spread like fingers from his wound and ran across his abdomen and down into his groin. Crestfallen, Jane witnessed men pass from wounds less grave, yet she would not give up.

One of the five men who helped her save Constantine approached her. "You have not eaten for days." He set a bowl of steaming broth beside her. "If you are to save him, you must keep up your own strength." Concern filled his face. "It will do him no good if you fall ill as well."

Jane thanked him but said nothing more as he joined his compatriots in the corner of the ruins. The rich aroma of the soup stirred her hunger and she ate a bit. But when Constantine's body jerked with another bout of the fever, she quickly forgot the food.

As she pressed cool cloth to his burning brow, she heard men speak grimly among themselves. They whispered that the rider sent out to get help had not returned, and their expressions showed they thought he must be dead or captured. She closed her eyes and prayed, unwilling to believe all was lost.

When night fell, the moon's light glistened across Constantine's face, painting it with a sickly pallor. The occasional flicker of his eyelids accompanied by shallow coughs told her that he barely lived.

It soon became clear to Jane that she could do no more. Only one person might be able to save him.

****

Cynthia huddled, shivering against the frigid night air and pulled at the ropes that bound her to the stout central pole in Simon's tent. Before they left for the trip back, he allowed her to bathe in the river and gave her a new gown to wear from among those he had collected from other women taken to Donahyde Castle. After a half-day's ride, he made camp and secured her fast to the tent post. But he had not allowed her to warm near a fire, making sure that she knew his will prevailed over her comfort. Then he left her alone to receive a courier from Leyborne Castle.

She had suffered the indignity of the ride slung across the rump of one of Simon's horses; a punishment he decreed would soften her resolve. Every bone in her body ached from the ordeal. Weary from all she endured, she fought to stay awake, but her battle seemed to be in vain as she rested her cheek against the rough wood and closed her eyes. Safe near her heart, she took comfort in the fact that at least Simon still had not found the amulet.

After what seemed like only seconds, she became aware of shouting and the sound of men moving quickly outside the tent. Torchlight exploded through the opening flap momentarily blinding her.

The ropes on her wrists cut into her skin as she turned her head away to shield her eyes against the brightness.

"What is it?" she asked, adjusting to the change in illumination. Simon stood before her, anger in his eyes. "Has something happened?"

Simon lowered his hand, his face hard. He spun and thrust the torch into a nearby brazier. "It seems that your minstrel does not have the good sense to die."

Cynthia reeled with the news, her heart racing with fresh hope. "What do you mean?" she asked, hiding her excitement. She watched Simon rage around the tent.

"My men intercepted a rider from the north. And after some," he stopped, his scowl deepening, "vigorous persuasion, he revealed he was on his way to Bramell to secure some herbs." He took two strides to her. "It seems your lady in waiting needs them to heal the minstrel's wounds."

Unable to contain the joy in her heart, Cynthia's voice filled with happiness as she rose to her knees. "You have failed," she said. "When Constantine recovers fully, no one will stop him from coming for me."

"Not if I find him first and finish what I had begun," Simon screamed, unfastening the ropes that bound her so roughly that he nearly broke the delicate bones in her wrists.

Cynthia bit down on her lip, refusing to cry out in pain.

"This time you will stand beside me and watch him die," Simon promised, his fury mounting. He jerked her arm, intending to toss her into the arms of a waiting guard, but Cynthia stiffened, refusing to be moved. In response, he bound her wrists once more and slung her across his shoulder. When he did, the amulet she protected so carefully dislodged itself from deep inside the bodice of her dress and fell to the ground.

The glint of gold caught Simon's eye. "What have we here?" he asked, tossing Cynthia to the guard like a bolt of fabric. He picked up the gleaming circle. Anger filled his eyes when he looked at her. "You've been hiding things from me."

Cynthia pressed her lips together refusing to confirm or deny the accusation.

Simon held the amulet between his thumb and forefinger, examining it closely. "The cross and red dragon. Markings of a knight." He thrust it at Cynthia. "Where did you get this?"

Again, Cynthia did not answer.

His brows furrowed and he looked at the charm more closely. "And what is this?" He rubbed his thumb across the metal. "Blood?" His gaze rose to capture Cynthia's eyes. Rage now raced across his face, further darkening his features and causing the muscles in his jaw to tense. He grabbed her chin with one hand and forced her face level with his. "Your minstrel is a Knight of Arthur?"

Cynthia wrenched free of his hand. "And he will bring you to the justice you deserve for taking what was never yours to have!"

Simon's fist closed around the pendant. "Leyborne belongs to me!" His gaze raked over her. "And so do you." His mouth curled in a sneer. He looked up at the cross beams of the tent before nodding to the soldier holding her. "Tie her fast."

Cynthia screamed as the soldier tossed a length of rope over one brace, looped it through her bindings and pulled until her arms stretched painfully above her head. Simon pulled on the ropes, checking the tightness of the knots and making sure she could not escape. He then dismissed the soldier with a wave of his hand.

Cynthia watched in horror as Simon removed his gloves. “Constantine will save me,” she said with conviction. “And when he discovers what you have done, you will be the one at the point of a sword.”

Simon looped the gloves through his belt. Your treacherous handmaiden will not be getting her heathen cures,” he said, triumph in his voice. “By the time she realizes that her messenger failed, it will be too late.”

“Nay, the Almighty will not let him die.”

“Look around,” Simon said, extending his hands and turned in a circle. “The Almighty has abandoned you.”

“I will pray he forgives your blasphemy,” Cynthia spat out at him before a blood curling scream escaped her as Simon silenced it with a hand to her mouth.

****

The sight of Cynthia helpless and bound almost undid his resolve. In her defiance, she was magnificent. His loins clenched. He could barely wait to have that magnificence writhing under him. He dragged himself back from the brink. He would not take her totally, but he would have a taste.

“You can pray all you want. In the morning, we go to your bridal bed,” he said.

Cynthia pulled at the ropes holding her. "You mean my tomb."

"Call it what you will. There you will lie in silence and darkness, bound and waiting for my beck and call." He cupped her breast with his hand, a smile curling as her nipple reacted through the thin fabric. "And I will call often, my love," he said, his thumb circle the rising bud.

She twisted away from his touch as much as he would allow it. "You disgust me."

"That will change once you have tasted what I will give and your minstrel is dead."

"Only a fool would kill one of Arthur's Knights in cold blood."

"The point of my sword makes no distinction between knight or troubadour. The next time he tastes its bite, I will not make the same mistake as I did the last time. He will die painfully and slowly as you watch."

"You will not have that chance. He will come for me," Cynthia said, her voice confident.

"I am counting on it," Simon spat back at her. "As a Knight of the Table, he will give me the advantage. I will use his over-blown sense of duty against him." His mouth curved in a cruel smile. "And you will be the bait I need to exact my revenge."

Simon pulled a dagger from his belt and sliced the bodice of her dress. Her breasts fell free into his waiting hands. His gaze stayed locked with hers as his fingers stroked and pinched her nipples to erection.

Cynthia fought him as best she could, but he merely laughed and took one of the rosy buds into his mouth while he held her tight against the pole with his hands. His arousal grew as he suckled and bit into her flesh with sharp teeth, but he smothered her screams of protest and took his fill of her with his mouth and tongue.

Chapter Fifteen

Jane crept toward the soldiers camped near the stream. When the rider had not returned, she knew she had to venture deeper into the forest to collect what herbs and medicines she could find in the woods to help Constantine. Her heart nearly stopped when she came upon the soldiers so close to where her small rebel contingent rested.

Risking discovery, she used the trunks of large trees for cover and came as close to them as she dared. Judging by the condition of their campsite, they had already eaten and were settling in for a few hours rest. They'd gathered around a small fire, drinking from their tankards and laughing at words she could not hear.

If she could get close enough, she might pick up on their talk. Maybe she could find out something about Cynthia.

Intending to keep to the edge of the forest, she hadn't gotten far when she rounded a tree and came face to face with a man. She had kept her gaze steadily on the camp and had not seen him. But now her approach surprised him. And he had surprised her.

She turned and ran but he gave chase and quickly caught her, yanking her by the arm and turning her to face him.

"What are you doing here?" he asked her.

Jane opened her mouth to speak, but her gaze snagged on the man in front of her. For a moment she could not move. His dark blond hair hung in waves around his handsome features. Eyes that rivaled the color of the bluest sky held her fast, the pull of his gaze running down to her bones. She willed her femininity not to react so carelessly to him and found her voice.

"I'm fetching some water from the stream," she said, warring again with her sensibility as her gaze returned to his eyes.

The man's gaze dropped to her empty hands. "Without a bucket?"

Hoping he posed no threat, Jane sought her escape. "I must have dropped it when you startled me." She turned to leave. "I best be getting back. They'd be worried about me."

He touched her arm, a touch as light as a breeze but one that affected her as though she'd be hit by lightning. "You should not be out in the woods alone. Let me escort you."

He began to walk with her toward the camp, but she stopped him. "Not there."

His face clouded. "I sense treachery here." His hand moved instinctively to the hilt of the sword at this side. "Your name, lady."

"It is Jane." She put her hand over his. "And it is not treachery, sir, 'tis hopelessness." She nodded toward the camp. "The soldiers there fly the colors of Lord Simon of Cowell, a most dangerous, evil man."

"So say you."

Jane saw one of the soldiers stir and look in the direction where they stood. She put a finger to her lips and urged him to move deeper into the forest.

Satisfied they were a safe distance from the camp, she stopped walking and turned to him.

"Lord Simon is a scoundrel. He nearly killed an innocent man and kidnapped the lady I serve. Even now men loyal to her make plans to free her. If we do not make haste, I fear he will force himself upon her if he has not already. I risk discovery to find healing herbs to save a man's life, a man he intended to kill."

His eyes searched Jane's face. For a long moment he seemed to ponder her words. His gaze roamed her from the tilt of her head to the tension in her stance. "Your eyes are filled with concern, lady. A deceitful person is careful not to show such emotion. I believe your claim to be true." He removed his hand from sheathed his weapon and nodded to her. "And I believe I owe you an apology."

"You owe me nothing," she countered. "But this delay may have cost my lady the life of her love."

The sound of approaching hoof beats cut his answer. When the rider saw them, he quickly reined his horse. "Jane!" he called out, dismounting. He ran to her side. "The minstrel, my lady. You must return to the cloister. He has taken a turn for the worse."

"No!" she cried. "Not when we are so close to freeing my lady and avenging a sin against righteousness!" She fell to her knees in sadness.

The man put his hands on her arms. "Who is this minstrel? Why is he so important to you?"

Allowing herself to be pulled to standing, Jane rose with the gentle pressure of his fingertips. "He is more than a minstrel. He is the love of my lady, Cynthia. I have seen the joy they bring each other. When Lord Simon ran a sword through his side and stole my lady away, it provided me with the reason to deliver justice both in the name of love and to settle an old score. But if Constantine dies, it will kill my lady as sure as if Lord Simon put a sword in her heart as well, and I will have failed them both."

"Constantine?" The name left the man's lips like a final breath and his face paled. "This man of whom you speak, the man who lies badly wounded, he came from the lands to the north and west?"

Jane's brows furrowed. "Yes. You know of him."

He nodded, his eyes filling with anguish. "He is the reason I have come. I am Braeden, Knight of Arthur, and he is my brother."

Chapter Sixteen

Cynthia dressed carefully in the sunny yellow gown that Simon provided for her. She knew what needed to be done. Simon had to drink the sleeping draught before he tried to seek comfort in her. She endured as much as she could under his hands last eve. She could endure no more. She had to escape. Tonight. Constantine was dying. She felt it. She needed to be with him and try to help save him.

Fortunately upon arriving back at Leyborne Castle, Simon isolated her in her old room. That was his first mistake. His second was leaving her there alone. She knew exactly where Jane kept her collection of herbs. She easily found the nightshade concealed behind a panel of the raised platform on which sat the bed. The deep pockets of her gown would suit well enough to conceal the herb.

She was ready when one of Simon's soldiers came for her. Her footsteps echoed hollowly as she approached his room. Before entering she paused and prayed for the strength to accomplish what must be done.

Simon waited until the soldier left before he spoke. "There's something you need to know," he said, gesturing for her to sit on the edge of his bed.

Positioning herself so she stood as far away from him as possible, she complied. "Is it about

Constantine?" She held her breath, preparing for the worst.

"I have decided to have him declared an outlaw and put a price on his head ensuring that he will be found. That is, if he still lives."

Cynthia blanched. An outlaw. The entire shire would become Simon's eyes and ears. She sagged against the bedpost.

Her stricken expression must have convinced Simon that she had accepted her fate and would not fight him. "It's now time to keep your part of the bargain." He looked around his room. "All the comforts are here as you requested."

He reached for her, but she quickly rose. Her mouth went dry. She needed time to think. The thought of his body on hers repulsed her, but she could not let him know. "I need time to prepare myself," she demurred. "The events of the past few days have been draining. Let us have some wine first. To relax." She dipped her head. "I promise to not disappoint you if you allow me this one small appeal," she said with half-closed lids.

"Very well," Simon settled back onto the large pillows at the head of the bed. "There are two pitchers of wine on the table. One apricot nectar, one red wine. Choose whichever you want."

Cynthia walked to the table and selected the nectar. The sweetness would help disguise any taste of the herb she would add. Turning her back to Simon, she reached inside the pocket of her gown and wrapped her fingers around the dried and powdered nightshade leaves. She sprinkled a generous measure into one of the cups on the table and filled them with the thick golden liquid. Then she returned to Simon's side and handed him the doctored drink. She forced her face to be devoid of any emotion as she watched him take a healthy gulp of the juice. She sipped hers and waited.

She watched in silence as Simon drained his cup before throwing it across the room. It shattered against the far wall with a loud crash. "Now," he said, lunging for her, "I will have you whether you are ready or not. I will be denied no longer."

Cynthia stiffened as he grasped her wrist and jerked her to him, pulling her down onto his bed. With a surge of strength she pushed him away. "Get off me," she demanded, her eyes blazing with fury. His touch brought back visions of the previous night, making her unable to continue with the charade. "You disgust me." She ran to the window and stepped up onto the stones making up its frame. She braced a hand on either side of the transom and turned to him. "I'd rather die."

"I should have known your submission was just part of an act," he accused. "You have played me for a fool." He rose and grabbed his sword. "If you wish to die, then allow me to assist you." He started toward her.

Cynthia rose on her toes and leaned back, intent on jumping before she would feel the sword enter her body when his eyes suddenly grew murky and a confused look passed over his face. In the next instant his eyes rolled upward and he dropped heavily to the ground.

Quickly Cynthia got down and walked to him. She jostled him where he lay and called out his name. He did not move. The potion had worked.

A wave of uncertainty washed over her replacing the relief she initially felt. Although she remembered what Jane used to make the soldiers sleep, she did not know how much to administer and feared that she may have killed him. Intrinsic compassion made her reach down and feel his neck for a pulse. She felt almost disappointed when a strong beat met her fingertips. He would sleep. But she had no idea for how long.

She picked up his dark cape from the floor next to the bed and wrapped it around her shoulders and headed for the courtyard. The moon had slipped behind a cloud deepening the shadows that lay in doorways. She made as little noise as possible as she quickly crossed the quad. Moments later she scrambled through the door in the castle wall.

Outside the castle the merchants who spent the day selling their wares to the townspeople had raised their tents a few yards away from the gate to settle for the evening. Earlier she heard two soldiers talking about them. The merchants were waiting until dawn to return to their villages. Their decision would be her salvation.

A line of horses tethered together for the night lined the stream next to the tents. If Constantine were to be declared an outlaw, she would soon join him as a horse thief.

She had just untied and mounted the smallest of them when one of the merchants came out of his tent and saw her.

“I need to borrow this fine steed,” she called out to him as she pulled on the reigns. “I promise you will receive payment when my task is done.”

Before the man could react, she started the horse into a gallop and rode off into the night.

****

Night had fallen when Braeden and Jane galloped into the courtyard of the church. News of Constantine's condition had encouraged them to ride like madmen to get to him.

One of the soldiers who remained with Constantine ran toward them when they dismounted. "I beg you to hurry, Jane."

Jane cast Braeden a worried look. New fears ran through her and she pushed past him, making her way to where the church dormitory once stood with Braeden fast behind her. She stepped into the crumbling room where they saw a group of men standing around Constantine who lay on a bed of straw and grass. The tallest of them stepped forward, his dark robe partially concealing the gleam of armor.

Braeden unsheathed his sword. "Step away from my brother," he ordered. He reached out to Jane and drew her behind him. "He wears the armor of a soldier."

"Draw down your sword, good knight," she replied. "Not all of Lord Simon's men are loyal to him and his evil ways. We have allies among them."

The soldier crossed the space between them, acknowledging the knight with a bow. "This man is your brother?"

Casing his sword, Braden looked over at his prone kin and watched Jane apply a cool cloth to his brother's fevered brow. "Aye. Younger by five years." He shrugged off his dusty cape and dropped to a knee at his brother's side. He reached out and touched Jane's arm. "Tell me. How did this happen?"

"A trap set by Lord Simon."

Braden's eyes filled with pain. "Will he live?" he asked.

Jane pressed her ear to Constantine's lips, then to his heart, listening for signs of life. Faint as they were, she held onto hope. "He fights the fever more than most men would. His life rests in his own hands now."

Chapter Seventeen

When dawn came, Simon's cry of disgust shook the stonewalls of Leyborne Castle.

"She has gone too far this time!" He took a step and swayed, the pain in his head exploding once more. His fingers pressed deeply into his temples. "The vixen tried to poison me. Guards!" he shouted.

As one, Simon's men-at-arms rushed into the room. "Sire?"

Simon lifted his head, "Where is she?"

"Gone," the captain said, standing tensely alongside his men.

Simon grabbed a bowl from a table near his bed and threw it across the room. "She will pay," he vowed. "Bring me a parchment and my seal." As one of the men hastened to comply, he swiveled to face the soldiers. "Captain, ready the army. We ride in an hour." Fire blazed in Simon's eyes. "We will search every village, turn over every blade of grass in England, if we must, but she will be found. Along with her lady in waiting and the minstrel. Let the word go out that anyone who helps or harbors them will be named an enemy of the state and will be executed."

"Sire," the captain said, bowing in respect to his lord, "we do not know to where Lady Cynthia has fled."

With a lightning quick motion, he reached into his belt a pulled out a dagger. With the flick of his wrist, it soared through the air, landing in the captain's throat. Eyes wide in fright, the man fell to the cold stone floor.

"Let that be the first lesson to all. My orders will be obeyed without question. I reserve no mercy for the weak." He walked to the fallen man and pulled the dagger free. "You," he said, ripping the captain's insignia from the shoulder of the man at his feet and tossing it to the solider nearest the door. "You are in charge now. Do you also question my command?"

"No my Liege," the soldier said, catching the crest midair. "The garrison will be ready."

"Sire, your scroll," the returning soldier said, handing Simon the paper, ink, a quill and his seal.

Simon ripped them from his hands and hastily filled the paper. After signing the document, he lit a candle, dripped wax on the bottom of the paper and pressed his hallmark onto it. Extending the document, he handed it to his new captain.

"Take this to the Bishop and have it recorded."

The captain nodded and took it from Simon's hand, catching a few words. "Sire?"

"A death warrant. For the she-devil who tried to kill me, the witch who supplied her with the poison and the rogue who set the plan into motion."

****

Cynthia rose hard and as fast as she could, relying on her heart and instincts to show her the way. She swung the horse around and headed north, riding between pine boughs. She remembered Jane talking about church ruins far beyond the town in a forest of pine trees where monks grew herbs and spices in the cloister gardens. She prayed the direction she was taking was true.

She hung on the reigns for a moment and then leaned across the horse's neck. "I promise you rest soon," she whispered to the mare. "But I must find Constantine."

She looked around as she rode, seeing only the blaze of darkness under an innocent moon. The brown mare pounded on for what seemed like hours. Throughout the frantic ride, she gripped the neck strap and clung to him like a burr.

The track the horse took opened enough for her to make out a well-traveled path that sliced its way uphill through the forest to a crest, where she thought she could see the glimmer of light in the distance. She pulled on the reigns and directed the mare to follow it. Soon the path plunged down hill again and she found herself splashing through a stream, fetlock deep. When the mare came out of the water, she continued alongside the water until she found a pathway beaten flat along level turf. There the horse suddenly pulled up and slowed to a walk.

In the distance Cynthia could hear horses riding at a fast trot. A man's voice briefly rose and then a flurry of torches came over the ridge to her right. The lead horseman saw her and barked an order. The troop turned, galloping quickly in her direction.

Cynthia's stomach clenched. She could not guarantee that she could outrun them; there were too many. But she had to try. She kicked the mare in the ribs and took off in a gallop. Water rose in a large splash as the horse jumped the stream nearly unseating her.

She rode faster. Turning to look over her shoulder, she could see that the soldiers were gaining on her. In desperation, she heeled the horse once more and begged him to go faster.

Seconds later the soldiers caught up and wheeled to either side of her. One reached out and grabbed the reigns of her horse, brining it to a stop. The horse fidgeted under the blaze of torchlight as the one of her escorts held onto the bit and led her back toward his officer.

In the yellow light, she could see the standard under which they rode, a scarlet dragon holding a cross. Hope and fear swirled inside her. She recognized it as the same crest on the pendant Constantine wore around his neck. Then she saw a familiar form astride a horse to the rear of the contingent.

Friar Joseph saw her and waved. Cynthia realized that the next few minutes would bring her either salvation with knights coming to her aid or despair with the dreadful news of a knight's death.

Either way, it seemed, her search for Constantine had come to an end.

Chapter Eighteen

Braeden studied Jane's silhouette as she worked over his brother. The fire burning nearby cast a warm golden glow over her, and he remembered the silken feel of her skin under his fingertips when he touched her. She reached into a bucket filled with water from the nearby stream to moisten the cloth she used to cool Constantine's brow. Droplets splashed onto her hand, making it sparkle in the moonlight. Surely The Almighty sent her as an angel sent to save Constantine.

He tore his eyes away from her to allow him to think clearly. Having ridden at a merciless pace to get here, he was exhausted. But no more than Jane, yet she tended his brother for hours without rest after their arrival.

Braeden shrugged off his dusty tunic, picked up one of the buckets set near the door and walked to the stream. There he filled it with water and lifted it above his head. The cool liquid splashed against his tired body, the cold jolt refreshing his aching muscles and reviving him to a degree. But it did nothing to soothe the unrest of his soul.

Heavy thoughts assailed him and he dropped onto to the crumbling vestige of a stone bench. Setting the bucket at his feet, he rested his forearms on his thighs and looked back at the church.

He never met a woman like Jane. One moment she was a fierce as any warrior, ready to do battle for a just cause, the next as tender as any lady, nursing his fallen brother with care and compassion. In the short time since he met her, he came to learn much about her by just her actions. She was loyal to her cause, steadfast in her principle, yet kindhearted and selfless. Unlike the spoiled, pampered and helpless women of court or the work-hardened, sullen women who toiled on the land, Jane was a woman who commanded and earned respect. Such a women he thought could never truly exist.

He donned his tunic and walked back to the room and leaned against the remnants of the doorway. As he followed Jane's movements with his eyes, he felt something stir inside his heart. He watched her grind herbs with a stone to make a healing tea and suddenly wanted to take her hand in his so he could massage her palm and give those precious hands rest. When she dropped the grindings into an iron pot suspended above the fire, he wanted to take her in his arms and clean the moisture from her forehead with his lips.

When she returned to his brother and raised Constantine's head in order for him to drink, Braeden straightened in response to the groan that escaped his brother's lips. He started toward her but then stopped when he saw her lower her head and move her lips close to Constantine's cheek. He watched her gently run her fingertips over his brow and whisper soothing words to him.

Braden suddenly wanted those lips on his skin, her hands on his brow. He turned his head away from the sight and closed his eyes, praying for forgiveness for his begrudging his brother Jane's healing ways in his time of need.

When he looked back, Jane was beside him.

"Is he any better?" he asked, disguising the tremor in his voice as best he could.

"He fights with the heart of a lion," she told him. "But even a lion weakens when wounded."

Braden noticed the bucket in her hand and reached for it. "I'll get more water." He retrieved another at his feet. "I'll fill both." He began to turn away when he felt her hand on his bare arm.

"I'll go with you. After the long ride, I'd like to wash a little. The men will stay with Constantine and come for me if there is any change."

His skin burned where her hand touched. He never felt this intense a reaction to any women before. Although he knew he shouldn't be alone with her, he would not, could not, refuse her. He tightened his grip around the rope handles of the buckets to keep himself from dropping them and running his hand through the dark mass of her hair. She folded her arms cross her chest and walked alongside him.

"Tell me more of this Lord Simon. Why do you hate him so?" he asked her.

"Lord Simon of Cowell is an evil land baron who takes what he wants through intimidation and death. He did so to all these lands," a sharp intake of breath followed her words, "and more."

Braeden glanced over his shoulder. "My brother, he challenged this lord?"

Jane smiled sadly. "No, he simply fell in love with one he was to free from an agreement of convenience."

Braeden stopped and turned to her. "Ah, the mystery clears for me then. I fought beside my brother in battle when a knight fell, mortally wounded. He charged Constantine to release his lady from a pact made by her father when she was a child. It was to be a simple charge, a noble charge." Braeden smiled. "But none considered a turn like this."

"Love happens when it happens," Jane offered as a wind came up, catching her hair and sending dark tendrils dancing across her face.

Braeden set down one of the buckets, reached up and brushed the silky curls from her cheek. "Aye," he agreed.

Jane noticed the cool breeze prickled Braeden's damp skin and saw his shoulders move with a shiver. "The night air chills you," she said lifting the hem of her tunic. She dabbed at the faint water droplets that still clung to his neck. "I won't have you also falling ill." She lifted her eyes and their gazes locked. Jane realized they had walked far from camp and were now completely alone. "Perhaps it would be prudent to warm yourself by the fire back at camp."

Braeden could feel the warmth in Jane's touch through the thin layer of cloth and his muscles vibrated beneath her fingertips. His eyes searched her face. "Yes, perhaps it would."

The bucket in his hand dropped to the ground. His strong hands moved up to cradle her face and he tilted his head to bring his mouth onto hers. Gently at first, then more deeply he kissed her. The restraint he had tenuously controlled when their lips first touched quickly disappeared, replaced by passion and hunger.

Jane shuddered and closed her eyes, allowing the sensation of his lips against hers, of his strong hands moving down to caress her neck, her shoulders, the small curve of her back to engulf her. She did not pull away, but instead clutched his shoulders and moved closer into him.

It's the danger taking control, Braeden's mind warned, you would never allow this if you were thinking straight. You are a Knight of the Round Table with a sworn an oath to serve and protect. Once this new quest is won, you must return to Camelot and to your king.

But he didn't care. If this is how Constantine felt when he kissed Cynthia, then Braeden finally understood why they had risked all to be together.

His arms surrounded her, wanting her to feel safe, protected. He kissed her ear, her cheek, her chin, and he knew without a doubt that she would be in his heart forever. In the mere breath of time he had come to know her, for the first time in his life he understood that there could be happiness for him with a family.

Her deepened his kiss and felt her retreat from his arms.

"Braeden, no, she said. "The black dragon still hunts us. I cannot afford to be distracted from what still needs to be done, no matter how pleasant the distraction might be." The tremor in her voice told him that she struggled to get out the words.

He raised his head from her lips and met her gaze. The naked desire filling her eyes only made him want her more. But he would not allow his needs before hers.

"I'm sorry." His voice heavy, as if the sheer effort of speaking taxed him.

She pushed on his chest and maneuvered out from his embrace. Grabbing a bucket, she scooped up some water and began walking back to camp. The two strides he was beside her. He put a hand on her shoulder, turning her to face him.

"Please. I apologize. I should have never taken such liberty."

She cut him off with a shake of her head. "It's all right. We are both weary," she said hoping her words reassured, though she could barely see his expression in the dim light. "We just have to be vigilant. I do not care to be surprised by an attack from some of Simon's guards, especially since Constantine's life still hangs in the balance."

Braeden's fingers flexed on her shoulders. "Perhaps then, when this conflict ends, we..." His head suddenly jerked upward. "Did you hear that?"

Jane's brow creased. "Hear what?"

Braeden spun on his heels, pulling her into the brush and behind a large tree. They were barely out of sight when the sound of the hoof beats of many horses filled the air. Horror froze her in place as she crouched behind the tree trunk. Braeden pulled her hard against him, his thickly muscled arms squeezing her against his body so she would not be seen.

Within seconds the horses were upon them. She felt Braeden shift, moving slightly away from her to see the oncoming troop. His hold on her relaxed and he stood, moving clearly into view.

"Hold," he called out, raising his arms and moving them back and forth above his head. He reached back and grabbed onto Jane's hand, pulling her out from behind the tree. "We are here!" The moonlight illuminated the banner furling high above the lead rider. A scarlet dragon holding a cross. The second rider came into view and Jane felt her heart race.

It was Cynthia.

Chapter Nineteen

Cynthia dismounted quickly and ran to Jane. “Where is Constantine?”

Tears of joy ran down Jane’s cheeks as she answered. “Thank God you have come. He’s here, in the cloister.” They ran together to the ruins. “It is grave my lady.”

Cynthia shuddered when she saw him, fear closing her throat. Grasping Constantine’s limp hand, she tried to steady herself, but a lump formed in her chest. His skin was so pale, his breath so shallow, that at first glance she wasn’t sure he still lived. She knelt beside him and pressed his hands to her heart, studying his face, wondering if she would ever see his eyes again.

“He is very weak,” Jane said. “I have done what I could.”

Cynthia stroked Constantine’s hot, dry brow. She sensed that he could feel her touch; his eyelids seemed to flicker just a little. She traced his cheeks with her fingertips and brushed the thick, blond hair behind his ears.

He lay with his head turned to her, his face still, but with a gray tinge to his skin that frightened her. And he seemed so thin. How could he have lost so much flesh in such little time. It seemed like every bone in his rib cage strained beneath the stained bandage that wound around his chest.

"Constantine, can you hear me?" she asked. "Don't leave me. Not now, not ever." She repeated the words over and over as though they alone would keep him alive and searched his face anxiously but there was no change.

"I fear his spirit has fled," Jane said. She placed a hand on Constantine's brow. "I fear it is far away."

"Tell me what to do to save him," Cynthia pleaded.

"We can do nothing more. But perhaps you can." Jane looked down at Constantine. "Talk to him. Call him back from the world between life and death."

"I will not leave him. Tell me how to minister the potions and teas."

Jane pressed her lips together and nodded. Quickly she instructed Cynthia on the healing art.

Cynthia steeled herself against her fears and took up Constantine's care. She changed his bandages, tried to get him to eat and drink, while she applied cool cloths to his brow. As the night came and the air grew cold, she lay down beside him to warm him with her body.

"I will call you if there is a change," Cynthia said, easing her arms around Constantine. "Please get some rest of your own."

"I will be just beyond the door," Jane assured, turning and leaving them alone. At the doorway she prayed that Constantine would not die this night in his lady's arms.

Outside, the men who rode with Cynthia had built a fire and were sharing a meager meal. Jane walked slowly toward them.

As soon as Braeden saw her, he rushed to meet her. "Has there been any change?"

Jane shook her head. "None. We can only hope that now that Cynthia is with him, it will make a difference."

"Jane," Gamel, who joined the cause upon hearing of Simon's attack on Constantine, called out. "Come join us. The food is hot and the meade is sweet. It will refresh you."

She declined with a polite shake of her head. "No, Gamel, I need to stay close to Constantine and Cynthia."

"He be a good man," Gamel said, shaking his head. "I be prayin' that he lives."

"As do I," Jane agreed. "As long as I have breath, I will not rest until either he rises or is taken by the Almighty."

"To do that, you need rest of your own. Come. Sit beside me. Lean on me for strength and solace," Braeden said, taking her elbow and leading her away from the group. "They will call if you are needed." He cleared some vines from a large boulder and gestured for her to sit. He stood behind her and placed his hands on her shoulders. "Let me try to relieve some of your distress." As gently as he could, he kneaded the muscles of her back.

Jane's head lolled forward and a sigh of fatigue escaped her lips. "There is magic in your hands, sir."

"I do not hold to such legends," he quickly said. Then his voice softened. "But if it would bring health to my brother, I would search a Druid's magic pouch for a cure," he replied.

Behind them laughter rose from the knights who joined the ragged group of loyalists protecting Constantine, and Jane turned briefly toward the sound. "'Tis good to hear that," she said. "The men need some pleasure to hold onto. They fight so bravely for such a cause nearly already lost."

"Never lost when hope still lives."

"The knights coming, finding Cynthia, finding us, is truly a miracle today."

"A miracle sent by the King," Braeden offered. He continued in reaction to the inquiring look on Jane's face. "As I came to look for my brother, long overdue in returning from his task, they came with a more serious mission."

The somberness on Braeden's face made Jane stand and touch his arm. "The pain in your eyes belies the calm in your voice." She swallowed hard, afraid of what he would say next.

"Arthur sent his knights to summon all those on personal quests back to Camelot. The Order of the Table is in grave danger. Lancelot and Gwinevere have betrayed the King and have brought turmoil to the realm. On the day of the queen's trial, Lancelot rushed the court and fled with her to France. Goodness and mercy have been replaced by du Lac's treachery and the Queen's deception. Even now Arthur masses an army to march to Joyous Guard to meet Lancelot in battle. At the next full moon, we fight to avenge an honor betrayed."

Jane lowered her eyes. "And you must go to join your king."

"Not yet," he said, placing his fingertips on her chin and raising her face to meet his gaze. "I have told the knights of your plight. The laws of chivalry say we cannot turn our backs on those oppressed. We will help you in your cause any way we can before we must leave for Camelot. But we must leave soon."

She turned and glanced back at the ruins, "Perhaps, if God wills it, your brother will rise and join you," she said.

"Aye," he agreed.

She placed her hands on his wrists and rose slowly, her palms gliding up his arms, feeling both strength and the tremor her touch produced. "You've just come and already you talk of leaving."

"Honor and a vow to the King makes it so, but my heart does not agree," he said just before his mouth descended upon hers.

****

The night came and then another dawn, but Cynthia refused to leave Constantine's side or to give up hope. She ate only enough to keep up her strength and slept only when forced by her weary body.

"Do you remember when I came to you?" she whispered so that only he could hear her. "How we pledged our love and wed our spirits that moment you loved me for the first time?"

He lay silent in her arms, but she continued.

"You lay me on the bed and removed my chemise and slipped it from my shoulders, looking at me like you were afraid to touch me." She smiled at the remembering. "But I looked into your eyes and knew I could trust you with my body and my soul. Remember, my love, that I then took your hand and kissed your fingertips. I placed your hand on my breast and felt you shudder as you touched me. My heart beat so wildly that I thought it would explode from my chest.

"Then you drew me against you. Your skin felt like fire to me as you lifted me onto the bed. You spread my hair across the pillow, and said it looked like fire lit silk.

"You touched me everywhere, in ways I could only have imagined before that day. My breath caught as a wealth of new sensations spread within me, yet I felt safe with you. Gently you lifted yourself over me. I knew there would be pain, but I knew it would only be for a moment. Then you kissed me as you lowered yourself and fit your body onto mine.

"I waited eagerly that moment of pain, that moment that would bring you to me and make us one. When you loved me fully for the first time, I cried out, suddenly afraid because I had never experienced a man's passion before. You stilled until your kisses calmed me and then we moved together, with the same rhythm, our bodies alive with pleasure and our souls alive with love. As I felt our passion peak, you cried out my name as we exploded together."

A tear came to her eye as she swore that he smiled. Holding him tightly, she let exhaustion overtake her, though she pulled against it. In the end, sleep won the battle and her body went limp beside his, her hand dropping his, breaking his bond to life.

Chapter Twenty

"Lady Cynthia!"

One of the men-at-arms shook her awake. Cynthia opened her eyes dispelling the mist of the wonderful dream she had been enjoying.

"The young noble, my lady." The man spoke with great difficulty, his bearded face lined with grief. "During the night, he..."

Cynthia's heart lurched and she turned toward Constantine, reaching out to touch his cheek. Instead of the fever that burned his skin, he felt so very cold. She heard a scream escape her throat. "No!" she cried, scrambling to her knees.

She pressed her ear to his lips, then his heart, searching for a sign of life. She felt as though she moved inside a nightmare from which she could not awake.

Hearing the scream, Jane and Braeden rushed into the room and to Cynthia's side. "Cynthia!" Jane's eyes widened as she read the horror on Cynthia's face. She dropped to her knees. "Constantine! No!" Her horrified gaze locked with Cynthia's. "Is he..."

Cynthia placed her hands on Constantine's chest willing his heart to beat strongly again. "If there is life still in his heart, it beats so faint I do not feel it." Tears streamed down her cheeks. "He came into my life only by the will of other men, finding me to tell me that I was free. But from the moment I looked into his eyes, I knew I would never be free of their memory. My love for him was sudden, urgent and pure. No matter what brought us together, I will not let us ever be apart." She closed her eyes and placed her hands on his wound. "You cannot leave me, my love. Until you smiled at me, I did not really live. You must smile at me again, for if you don't I will be condemned to a life in darkness."

Careful not to break her connection to him, with her left hand still pressed to his side, she took Constantine's right hand in hers and pressed it to her heart. Lifting her eyes, she prayed. Braeden fell to his knees beside Jane, and they joined her.

"Simon hunts us, my love," Cynthia continued. "He hunts us because he fears us."

"Does he stir?" Braeden asked.

"No, but he hears me," Cynthia said. "I know he does."

"Then keep talking to him," Braeden urged. "Bring him back from the abyss of death on which he perches."

"Lord Simon knows you are a knight. He knows that my love belongs only to you. And he knows that should you meet, he will fall, not you. You must heal. Together we can free Leyborne shire from his madness." Her lips touched his brow and she willed him to live with every ounce of strength she possessed.

Suddenly she thought she heard a breath escape his lips. Dare she wish it to be so? Hope rippled through her and her breath came in short pants.

"Breathe, my love," she begged him, her mouth on his. "Come back to me."

As her tears fell on his cheek, a sound, half cry, half gasp escaped his lips. His chest rose fully for the first time in days, filling his lungs with cool, sweet air at last. His eyes opened and he whispered her name.

"Cynthia. I will never leave you," he said with great effort, his voice only a whisper.

Now tears of joy streamed down her face as she covered Constantine's mouth fully with hers. Gently he returned her kiss and she knew that all would be well.

****

The village was afire. People fled screaming from their cottages, covering their mouths against the heavy smoke that hung in the air. Fire shot through roofs and flames licked at almost every wall.

Lord Simon brought his sword down in a wide arc, cleaving the farmer's crude hoe in two and hurling him backward. He spat a bloody oath as the farmer's son, eyes wild in fright, pulled the older man away from another swipe of Simon's sword.

"Where are they?" Simon shouted at them.

A youth, blood streaming down his face from a gash on his forehead, rushed to Simon. "Sire, we don't know the people you search for. I beg you, leave us in peace."

Simon grabbed the young man by the scruff of his neck and tossed him down to the ground. He placed his boot on the lad's chest, laughing at the boy tried to lift the weight that pressed on him. Simon stood immobile as the boy gasped for air.

"By the blood of my father," the farmer shouted, "Leave us be. We are but poor sheep farmers. We harbor no criminals."

Simon kicked the helpless youth in the side and walked away from him. As the boy struggled to his feet, Simon raised his arm, his sword gleaming menacingly in his hand in the sunlight. "What I say now will be a lesson to anyone who shelters and aides the outlaws." The sounds of the clash going on around him quieted and a silence, infinitely more ominous, rose. "Captain," Simon called out, "gather the townspeople and bring them here."

From in the midst of the fighting, a tall man pushed forward. He saluted his lord with a bloodied weapon and ordered the soldiers to circle what was left of the villagers.

As Simon approached, the encircled men shouted and pushed against the arms that restrained them. The women wailed and begged for mercy. Impassive, Simon lifted his chin. "Choose one," he said flatly to the Captain of the guards in a voice that sounded like the grinding of heavy stones. "Then kill him as a warning to any man, woman or child who may try to assist the fugitives." He looked around the simple village. "Then, if anything remains. Burn it."

****

As the sun began to set, Cynthia nodded to the now familiar guard stationed just outside the crumbling walls of the church. The warm glow of the fire spread warmth across Constantine's sleeping face. He grew stronger every day, and each day she thanked the Power much greater than any for allowing him to live.

In the western sky she could see a large plume of smoke rising. She closed her eyes and prayed it was not another village being plundered because of her. Accounts of the cruelty of Lord Simon's raids were almost a daily occurrence.

Although they searched daily for Simon and his men, Sir Braeden and his knights did not find them to engage them in a final battle. The time quickly approached when they would have to ride with Arthur to Gaul and bring Lancelot and Gwinevere to justice. And Constantine would be asked to make a choice. She knew that.

Both Constantine and Braeden pleaded with Cynthia and Jane to join them, and though Cynthia gave Jane the freedom to choose her own path, Jane would not leave. And Cynthia would not leave the people who suffered on her account. Both refused the safe passage.

She would also not ask Constantine to stay with her. He had sworn an oath to Arthur and the Round Table, and his destiny lay there.

She pressed the heels of her hands over her eyes. She would surrender to Simon, but not until Constantine left. If he knew what she planned to do, he would defy the King's order and become a traitor to save her. She could not allow it. And he must also not be distracted in the fight against Lancelot at Joyous Guard. She would pretend all would be well, even if it meant never seeing Constantine again.

Tears burned her eyes. It appeared that Simon had won and her days with her love appeared numbered after all. She sat against the stone wall and encircled her legs with her arms. Then leaning her head on her knees, she let the tears come. Better she deal with her sorrow now, than when she would watch Constantine ride away to join his King at the fight.

Her anguish lay like a great weight on her chest. As she fought to smother the sobs that lodged in her throat, she didn't hear Constantine come up beside her. When he knelt down and touched her hair, she jerked her head in surprise. Without saying a word, he pulled her into his arms. She quieted instantly though her chest continued to heave and her breath came in short gasps.

"I didn't mean to wake you. You should rest," she said.

"It's all right," he whispered.

"I don't know why I'm crying," she lied.

His mouth tilted in a sad smile. "I do." He turned his face to hers, the corners of his eyes puckered with weariness. "I wish you would come to Camelot with me. You would be safe there."

She shook her head. "I will not run away and leave the people who have defied Lord Simon to his cruelty. I will be safe enough in the forest until you come back for me when the battle is won."

"I will not leave you."

"You must."

"I came here to free you. My task still lays undone and a greater task looms."

She allowed her fingers to drift over his forearm alive with warmth and life. Had really been so close to death only a few days earlier? "No, you have freed me. You took anyway my loneliness and saved me from a prison from which I could never escape."

He dropped his forehead against hers. "But in doing so, we may have made a prison just as inescapable. My King declares war on a traitor who fled across the sea like a coward, and you still have need of my brother and his knights. I will not choose. There must be a way to end this."

Cynthia did not hesitate. "You must go to Gaul. I will not allow you to defy an order of the King."

"As a Knight of Camelot, I am also charged by King Arthur to be a champion for the ladies and damsels and fight their quarrels. Right must be protected against might when the cause is just. How can you ask me to leave you here at the mercy of a madman and still fulfill the responsibility of a Knight?" He reached over to her, running his fingers along the curve of her cheek and then tucking a curl of hair behind her ear. "I love you, Cynthia. Don't ask me to do this."

His touch was gentle, but the seriousness of his expression sent her heart plummeting. "I love you with all my heart, Constantine, but Camelot lies in turmoil and the King faces war with Lancelot at Joyous Gard. I would rather live a thousand years with Simon than have you tried for treason by the King to forfeit your life or live even one day in a dungeon for ignoring his call to arms. I have loyalists who will harbor me until you return. And while I wait for that day, I will love no other man but you."

Chapter Twenty-One

Jane finished washing in the stream and retraced her steps to the cloister. The night was peaceful. Too peaceful. She shivered as a premonition of warning raced up her spine.

All her life she had episodes of intuitive knowledge. Tonight's was the strongest yet. Suddenly she recalled her mother, two summers before she left, standing in the garden of their home in Wareham. Her mother had renounced her Druid order and the practice of the old ways, for a life with her father, but still dabbled in the arts when she could. As a child, Jane gathered with her mother in secret to learn the mysteries of nature that helped save Constantine's life.

Braeden's face materialized in her mind. Her attraction to him was strong, stronger than it had been for any man. She was almost sure she was in love with him. She could not remember all the words her mother spoke, but some now swirled in her mind—*I swear by the law of the order to hold above all else the right to love freely and compassionately for one's own sake.* Never did these words ring more true than they did now.

Did she dare profess her love to a Knight of the Round Table and ask him to accept a woman, who once noble, now could only live as a mere peasant to protect herself from discovery? Would he even believe that in the span of mere days, love could take root so deeply that she knew it would never leave her heart? A nervous laugh escaped her throat and sadness filled her. Of course he wouldn't. Knights carry the silken colors of Courtesans and Noblewomen into battle, not the coarse cloth of those who serve them.

She inhaled deeply to try to banish the heaviness from her heart. She walked toward the tent that had been raised for her a short distance away from the main ruins to afford Cynthia and Constantine some privacy in the main church. As she approached it, the strange apprehension engulfed her once more. Warily she looked around, but saw nothing to cause her the edginess she felt at the stream, She ducked inside the tent, secured the flap and froze. She was not alone.

She sensed his presence moments before his arm encircled her waist and he swept her into his arms. "Braeden."

His mouth came down on hers, taking her breath in a deep drugging kiss that proclaimed his need for her, answering all her questions and banishing her fears.

****

Cynthia lay in Constantine's arms, slipping in and out of a reverie of wonderful dreams. He stirred and she stretched in response, opening her eyes. When she did, her sudden gasp made Constantine rise and reach for his dagger.

Standing in the collapsing stone entry, framed by the remnants of the massive doorway stood the commander of one of Simon's most notorious and deadliest garrisons. His countenance was stern and even in the moonlight she could see the light of arrogance plain in his eyes.

With the sound of Cynthia's distress, Constantine sprang to his feet. "Who are you and how did you get passed the guards," he said assuming a defensive posture.

Cynthia stepped in front of him and placed her hand on his chest. "Put away your weapon. This is Captain Monfort, commander of Simon's first garrison. If he wanted us dead, we would be."

The soldier took a step forward as Constantine lowered his dagger but did not sheath it. "Lord Simon knows you are here, and sent me with a message," Monfort said.

Cynthia pressed closer to Constantine, his apparent disquiet heightened her own. A great clamor rose as her allies filled the room, ready to defend. Jane and Braeden pushed to the forefront.

"Brother, he did not harm you?" Braeden shouted with the heat of anger.

"No," Constantine assured. "He comes with a message from Simon of Cowell."

"Then say your message quickly," Braeden demanded of Monfort, his arm tightening protectively around Jane. "Before a wayward blade finds your throat."

"The lands to the west and the south now lie in ruin by Lord Simon's hand and the might of his warriors," Monfort stated plainly. "Even now the Village of Croton, just to the east, burns, and its townspeople scattered to the four winds."

Cynthia gasped in response, deaf to the commotion from the men around her.

"Along the river," Captain Monfort continued, "the farmsteads smolder and women bewail the loss of their men. The earth runs red with the blood of the dead. Now Lord Simon comes for you."

Constantine stood silent, his face drawn in lines of outrage. He reached for his sword, but Cynthia stopped him with a hand to his wrist. "Go and tell Simon..."

"There is more!" the captain shouted in blatant arrogance. "You are commanded to surrender. To me. Tonight. Lady Cynthia will return to Leyborne Castle and will become his concubine after paying proper tribute to his generosity. And you, minstrel, will be taken to Donahyde Castle to live out the rest of your life in chains." His gaze raked across the faces of those who joined the fight against Lord Simon. "The rest of you are of no consequence. Lay down your weapons and go. If you fail to do so, you will all surely die. Simon will sweep down into this cloister, descending down upon you like a lion chasing its prey and there will be no one among you who can stop him."

Braeden leapt forward, drawing his blade. "Brother, let me skin this worthless barbarian and send his hide back to his dog of a master."

Constantine silenced his brother with an imperious gesture. "Go," he said to the captain. "Tell Simon that as long as I continue to draw breath I will not allow him to lay a hand on Lady Cynthia. His fight is with me, and I will not yield to a madman, nor will I allow him to take my lady for his whim and pleasure. If it is war that he wishes, then he will find it here. He will find his tribute in arrows," Constantine shouted, his face livid with outrage. Raising his arm he balled his fist. "Now go, before the first arrow of tribute finds its mark amid Simon's crest on your chest."

"Breathe your last then," Monfort laughed ruthlessly. Spinning on his heels, he strode from the cloister.

Braeden placed a hand on Constantine's shoulder. "It seems we will wage two wars before we settle our hearts. You must rest, brother. Tomorrow comes swiftly and we shall have our first battle soon enough."

Chapter Twenty-Two

Constantine bolted awake at the sound of horsemen entering the cloister and men calling his name. He rose quickly and ran to the courtyard, Cynthia, Jane and Braeden following close behind. Two riders, their armor covered with dust, dismounted from tired steeds.

"What news?" he asked, anxiety lacing his voice.

"Simon has left camp and even now approaches," one of them said.

"How many?" He motioned to one of his allies for water and offered it to the riders. They drank long and hard.

"Two garrisons," the other replied. "Easily a thousand men, mostly on foot."

The gathering knights and soldiers rumbled at the report, each man realizing how narrow the possibility of defeating so numerous an enemy grew to be.

Constantine lowered his head in thought before addressing the men. "Now is the time," he shouted lifting his chin in a gesture of spirit, "time to prove that the sacrifices of those who gave their lives to protect us was worth the price needed to be paid." His face suddenly lit as a moment of clarity rushed through him. "Here's what we must do." He gave the men their orders, then place a hand on Braeden's shoulder. "If God is with us, the predawn mist will hide our small number," he said with a thin smile. "It is our only hope of surprise."

The camp burst into activity and at the center of it all, Constantine, Cynthia, Jane and Braeden stood, their eyes turned to the west, toward the enemy and their destiny.

****

From his place hidden in the trees, Constantine watched the stream run through the narrow ravine like a blue ribbon. The high hills surrounding the valley would be both a curse and a blessing. He understood all too well that although where he had positioned his allies made an ideal trap for Simon and his army, it also could make a tomb for his warriors. The only escape lay behind him through a range of low hills where most of his supporters now lay concealed.

Jane and Cynthia stayed well back, out of sight and out of danger with a small contingent of men ready to spirit them to Camelot should the battle go badly. He took a deep breath. At least they would be safe. He could not be sure Braeden and his knights were ready, but he knew he could not change the battle plan now.

One of the knights near him called softly and pointed. Constantine saw the first vanguard of Simon's troops appear from the west. A thousand strong, their dark mass formed a deadly wall bristling with spears and swords.

As the enemy force surged forward, Constantine prayed for his allies as his plan unfolded. Silently at first, but then with a growing roar of pounding hooves that sounded like faraway thunder, Braeden, his knights and a small contingent of supporters charged from their hiding place. Two hundred lancers and swordsmen pounded into the unsuspecting flank of Simon's column, smashing a wedge into the force. A swathe of Simon's army fell beneath the charging horses, lance tips piercing their armor.

"Quickly," Constantine shouted to the remaining men. "We must strike now before Braeden's men are cut to ribbons."

Trumpets blasted and a moment later, Constantine's forces began their charge. Constantine spurred his horse into a relentless gallop, pounding down the long slope toward Simon's army as archers loosed a whistling cloud overhead.

He leveled his sword, couching it ready as he drew nearer the enemy. His breath came in short gasps, every nerve alive with tension, and the sound of his heartbeat seemed to fill his helmet with thunder.

The clash came as a gigantic crash when the first of his factions rode headlong into the sea of Simon's men, sending length of razor sharp sweeps into the line of battle. Constantine and Braeden fought beside each other. Blows rang against their armor and clamored against their shields. They fought for what seemed like hours until finally the tide of battle began to turn to their favor.

Constantine lowered his sword and sighed bitterly at the sight of the battle as sporadic skirmishes broke out around him. His armor was covered with blood and bodies lay strewn on the ground as far as the eye could see. Behind him someone yelled and he turned in time to see Ranulf coming toward him, the axe he held with both hands ready to descend. Ranulf was too close; Constantine had little time to defend himself.

"We meet again, knight," Ranulf said, his initial blow deflected by Constantine's sword.

"So it seems," Constantine acknowledged. Bringing his sword forward in a wide arc, the stroke blocked by Ranulf's axe.

"His lordship will reward me when I bring him your head," Ranulf countered.

"You can try," Constantine chided with a series of drives.

The rebuke seemed to renew Ranulf's resolve as he wielded his axe in a series of blows that forced Constantine to retreat. His foot hit the body of a fallen comrade and sent him to the ground. A toothy grin appeared on Ranulf's face and he wheeled the great axe over his head, swinging it across in a blow that would surely cleave Constantine in two if it struck when suddenly the man's dark eyes widened and he stopped. Like a falling tree, he slumped forward onto the ground. In his back, an arrow, perfectly aligned with his heart, had pierced his mail, a great crimson tide erupting across his back.

When Constantine's gaze rose from his felled adversary, Jane stood ten yards away, her bow raised. She nodded to him and then turned, loading her bowstring and sending more arrows into the fray.

"Braeden," Constantine called to his brother. "Your lady does not wish to be away from you."

The sounds of battle filled the air, none louder than the sound of Braden's sword meeting metal. He glanced toward Constantine before his blade found the arm of a charging enemy and then to Jane, who was fighting with courage that belied her femininity.

"I'll be fine," Constantine said in response to the look of anxiety on Braeden's face. "Go to her."

With a yell that reaffirmed his resolve, Braeden ran toward Jane, slashing any enemy soldier he met in his path with unrestrained anger. When he reached her, he positioned himself so their backs touched to afford her as much protection as he could.

"Where are the men sent to guard you?" he asked as an arrow from her bow whistled by his ear and found its mark in the chest of a charging horseman.

"Guarding a tree draped in my cloak, I imagine," she replied, ducking under the raised arm of one of Simon's guards and pulling a dagger from her belt. Before she could use it, Braeden sent the man to the ground.

"And Cynthia?"

Jane tossed her head toward Constantine. "At your brother's side."

Braden turned in time to see Cynthia thrust a lance into a soldier's leg, giving Constantine the time needed to finish the fight. As another soldier engaged her, Braden watched her fight fearlessly. A worthy equal for his brother, Braeden thought, sure his brother needed no other help and turning his attention back to Jane. As is my lady for me.

"Call the men," he heard Constantine shout, after a short stretch of fierce battling. "The day is ours. We have beaten back the horde."

Braeden lowered his weapon and captured Jane in his arms, wanting to protect her from any stray rogue that may try for final vengeance. Together they watched Simon's minions flee out of the valley in full retreat before joining Constantine and Cynthia.

"Why so grim, brother? He asked once at Constantine's side. "Simon has been defeated. The people are free."

"Nay," Constantine replied. "We were betrayed. Simon did not fight in this battle. He sent his garrison to weaken us." He looked at his troops, weary and bloodied from the long fight. "I fear that the real fight comes soon."

Chapter Twenty-Three

Constantine lay back on the makeshift bed and watched Cynthia tend his wound. He winced, more with feral desire than with pain, as she gently wiped a cloth soaked in the feverfew tea Jane made earlier over the small section on his side that had reopened during the battle.

"Does it hurt still?" she asked him, dabbing at the dried blood that caked the red line in his skin.

"Not much." He reached out and moved the silken strands of blond away from her face. "Your touch disturbs me more."

Cynthia looked up from her work. "But I must do this. The cleansing properties of the brewed herb will lessen the chance of the infection returning. You fought bravely and with such passion, that we feared the wound would make you fall again." She dropped the cloth into the bucket at her side and cupped his face with her hand. "I cannot lose you a second time."

"It's not the healing that stirs me." Constantine covered her hand with his and squeezed it gently before moving it to his lips. He kissed her knuckles before running his tongue across her skin. "Come closer, my love."

She lay beside him, his shoulder a cradle for her head. Running her hand across his abdomen, her fingers barely touching him, she could feel him tremble. She traced the line his finely honed muscles made across his upper body and heard his breath catch when she entangled her fingers in the dark hair on his chest. Her heart beat faster as, with a boldness that astounded her, she encircled his manly nipple with her forefinger. Everything about being with Constantine felt so right, and she raised herself up on her elbow to look into his eyes to see if he felt it too.

His gaze did not disappoint.

"Cynthia," he said, his voice thick with desire, "I loved you from the first moment I saw you."

"Truly?" she whispered against his lips.

"Truly," he affirmed, entwining his fingers in her hair and taking her bottom lip between his teeth and tugging gently. "And each time we are together, I only want you more." He rose to his knees, pulling her with him. "Cynthia," he said, his voice thick with passion. "If Simon comes tonight, it would be better if you were not here."

"If Simon does come, his sole purpose will be to kill us and I would rather die in your arms."

Constantine raised his eyes to the heavens. "Then before the Almighty, and the souls of whatever saints or sinners reside among these ruins, I take you as my wife." He took her hand and kissed its palm. "If you will have me."

The silver glint of unshed tears shown in Cynthia's eyes. She leaned forward and rested her forehead on his. "Aye, my love," she said against his mouth before capturing his lips in a passionate request of her own. She pressed him closer to her, her breasts brushing his chest and her hips moving against his in a rhythm of invitation.

They eased back onto the bed, still wrapped in each other arms. Turning, Cynthia straddled him. As she slid her body down the length of his, he groaned. "If this be our last night on this earth, we will spend it together," she said between kisses. "Come, my husband," she whispered, her voice thick with want, "the wedding night awaits us."

Constantine's will shredded with her touch, driving him past the point of rational thought. All he could focus on with Cynthia. The feel her of hips on his, the softness of her hair brushing his skin as she moved, and the pleasure of the taste of her mouth on his.

In one smooth motion, he turned, capturing her body now beneath his. His hands tugged at the hem of her dress so he could feel her bare skin as he kissed her fiercely, demandingly. He reveled in the feel of her body beneath his hands and knew he would never want another woman as long as he lived.

If indeed they would draw their finals breath tomorrow then, he vowed, he would show her a glimpse of what Heaven might be made by their love this night.

The fire inside him blazed out of control but he stripped her slowly, adoring her with his lips as each article of clothing he removed. He ripped his own clothing from his body much more quickly, tossing it aside. Once they both lay naked, he rolled so now he was on his back, Cynthia atop him.

"Careful, my love," Cynthia whispered as she leaned over him, her hair brushing his thighs. "Your wound is still healing."

"It is enough for the dance of our love," he said.

His shaft rose high and hard as if begging for her touch. She smiled and let her fingers skim him. His breath caught and his body jerked at the touch.

"The first time we joined you said it was for me. This time, it is for you," she whispered, closing her fingers around his erection.

Her fingers caressed, swirling with an erotic touch that made him shudder. She traced his length with the palm of her hand before encircling him with her hand. The slow caress she began made his body go rigid, his fingers clenching the cloth covering the straw on which he lay.

She could hear his ragged breathing and saw him arch in time to her strokes. Even as her own womanhood clenched, wanting a release of its own, Cynthia took her pleasure in watching Constantine go mad beneath her touch.

Suddenly, he caught her bottom. "I can stand no more," he growled as he rolled and brought her beneath him. His fingers slipped between her thighs as his mouth kissed a paths to her nipples. His tongue teased each in turn before he took one fully in his mouth, sucking in time to his probing fingers until he heard her moan and beg for release.

Sure he could wait no longer, he plunged himself deep inside her. With a sharp intake of breath, she arched against him, her fingers digging into the muscles of his shoulders. His eyes held hers, the promise contained there clear.

He drove harder into her and she met him stroke for stroke. She moved her head from side to side on the bed as each stroke he made brought her closer to the edge of madness. He kissed her neck, tasting a small trickle of sweat he found there before suckling the skin to rosy red. As pleasure rolled through her in sweeping waves and her body shuddered. She arched fully and cried out his name.

Constantine captured her mouth with his as he drove into her once more, his body convulsing with the force of his climax as he filled her. His body still shivered in the aftermath of their love when he collapsed beside her, their breaths mingling.

She slipped her arms around him and kissed his forehead, watching as he drifted off to sleep. If this be the last time they loved, then they would take the joy of their union with them into eternity.

****

The sun barely began to show in the horizon when Cynthia woke to the distinctive sound of arrows slicing through the air and horse's hoofs pounding the ground.

"Constantine! Cynthia! Quickly!" Braeden shouted from outside the walls. "He comes!"

Constantine and Cynthia donned their clothes and ran to the courtyard. She shook her head in disbelief when she saw that men once again fell defending her, crimson-shafted arrows protruding from their bodies at all angles.

"It's a pity that I failed to end your life when I had the chance," Simon said from his mount, his tone thick with contempt.

"The chance now belongs to me," Constantine countered. "You should not have come. Your anger caused you misjudge us. I knew you would try to attack us at dawn, and I let you come." His smile widened. "I was ready this time."

Suddenly as if by enchantment, a dozen men, crossbows at ready, swarmed around them.

Constantine took a step forward as Simon's guards lowered their weapons to surrender.

"Now you will bring me to justice at Camelot," I suppose," Simon mocked.

"That is a privilege you do not deserve," Constantine returned icily. "Your crimes judge you. You do not even consider all that have died by your hand and how many families have suffered." He choked back a wave of emotion. "The damage you have done will take years to repair."

"How sweetly your display touches me," Simon said. "I do what is necessary to further my cause, not the cause of Camelot. Mordred has challenged Arthur for the throne and he will prevail." Simon's perverse laugh echoed, as he slipped his thumb under a length a cord at his neck. "Knight of Arthur," he mocked, raising the pendant so Constantine could see it. "This trinket belongs to me as a spoil of a war that comes."

"You are mad," Constantine said, shaking his head. "You do not deserve to wear what is given in honor by the true king."

"Take it from me then, minstrel."

Constantine raised his sword in challenge. "That and more I will do. Dismount and face the King's justice here."

Simon complied. The crossbows leveled at his heart afforded him no choice.

"Now draw your blade," Constantine ordered, pushing Cynthia into the protective arms of Braeden.

"No!" Cynthia broke free and gripped his shoulder.

"He must pay for what he has done, Cynthia. Now. By my hand."

"No!" she repeated. "Not now. Not by you. Let the court of Camelot judge him. I thought you dead and you just retuned to me." The words tumbled from her lips. "Do not place yourself at the end of his sword once again."

"The King prepares for war. In times like this, he charges his knights to administer righteousness, and that I will do. I love you with all my heart and soul, Cynthia." He touched her cheek. "But I cannot allow Simon to live a moment longer without atoning for the evil he has wrought." Gently he pushed her away.

Braeden rushed to him. "Brother, let me. You are still weak from your wound and the battle."

"No," Constantine said firmly. "My honor will be satisfied as will the King's justice when I am victorious in single combat." His gaze swept Braeden first and then his men. "By your word, do not intervene. Right must overcome might if the ideal of Camelot will live on." First Braeden, then each member of the troop nodded his acknowledgement. Constantine shifted back to Simon. "Let us cross steel, Simon of Cowell."

Simon tore his sword free with a snarl and leapt toward Constantine. The thrusts of his blade flashed like the play of lightening first toward Constantine's legs and then slashing upward. Blue sparks exploded as Constantine locked blow upon blow with his sword.

Cynthia watched in horror as the two men fought, growling from the fury of their strokes. Terror raced through her as Simon's blade ripped across Constantine's thigh. Blood mingled with sweat, but they fought on. The sound of steel against steel seemed only to fuel their ferocity.

Constantine pressed Simon with a series of powerful lunges, barely pulling his sword back before initiating another drive. The men locked blades for a tense moment before Simon twisted his wrist, smashing the hilt of his sword against Constantine's' temple and smashing a fist into his wounded side.

Reeling from the pain, Constantine stumbled backward, his hand releasing his sword as he fell to his knees. Somewhere in the back of his mind he heard Cynthia scream.

Tearing a whip that was fastened to his belt, Simon was on him in a heartbeat. The lash encircled Constantine's neck in a tightening embrace.

"Feel my answer even as your body struggles for air, minstrel," Simon hissed in Constantine's ear. "You were a fool to engage me once again. I will yet have Cynthia as my consort. And so not look for assistance from your band of rogues. Even now more of my men come."

Constantine heard shouting and became marginally aware of men engaging Braeden and the others in combat. No one could help him now. He fought against the darkness that threatened to descend upon him. His lungs burned for air and his pulse pounded thickly in his temples.

If he died by Simon's hand, then Cynthia would be at Simon's mercy. The thought of Simon lying with her made a powerful tide surge though him, giving him new strength. Rage at the thought of Cynthia submitting to the perverse will of the madman exploded within him, propelling him to his feet. He could not let Simon destroy his love.

Constantine thrust his head backward, feeling the snap of bone as it connected with Simon's nose. In response Simon let loose the whip and Constantine's body heaved uncontrollably finding air at last. Struggling to steady his feet, he saw Simon on the ground, blood streaming from his face. Still gasping for air, Constantine stepped back and stumbled over the hilt of Simon's blade.

Sensing an opportunity, Simon sprang forward, scooping up his sword from the ground. The two men collided in a thunderous crash. Constantine rolled to his knees, searching for something with which to defend himself as Simon descended upon him.

"Constantine!" Cynthia cried out.

He turned in time to see her toss him his sword. Catching it by the hilt and with a forceful shout, he raised it and sent it forward in a powerful thrust. It found its mark in a soul as dark as night. Simon's body crumpled and his breath left him in a slow hiss.

Constantine rose on unsteady legs. Grasping the sword with both hands, he used the last ounce of strength that remained to withdraw it from Simon's body. With shaking fingers, he then grasped the leather cord around Simon's neck and ripped it free.

He turned to Cynthia. "It's over..." His eyes rolled up and he fell backward onto the ground.

Cynthia rushed to him, cradling his head to her breast, tears of relief coursing down her cheek. "Yes, my love, it's over," she whispered, stroking his face and watching the anger and strain that marked his handsome face in battle slowly recede. "We are free."

Chapter Twenty-Four

The gardens of Leyborne Castle never looked so beautiful, Cynthia thought as she sat on the stone bench among the lavender. Everything seemed more vivid, more vibrant without the dark shadow Simon once cast on everything he touched.

Cynthia could hear the clatter of armed men in the courtyard beyond, but the sound no longer made her stomach clench in fear. This was her home now. Constantine delivered Sir William's final wishes; the ring and will recorded by a visiting Bishop. She was free of the promise made by her father and had been declared legal mistress of the Castle and its lands. No one would challenge a communiqué brought by a Knight of the Round Table.

Leyborne Castle was a grand manor, indeed, but it would be a prison without her beloved Constantine.

She looked up and saw him standing at the gate. In three great strides, he crossed the garden and took her into his arms. Even as he crushed her to him, it seemed that his arms were already letting her go. She pressed her lips against his as his hair fell across her cheeks and mingled with her tears.

"I cannot bear that you are leaving me," she whispered.

He looked down at her. "I must." He wiped her tears with his fingertips, forcing a smile onto his lips. "The King has declared war and we must join him in the battle. But I will come back to you. I swear it."

Constantine meant his words to be easy and reassuring, but she felt such disquiet in her heart. "I fear you will be away longer than I can bear."

His gaze raked across her lips. "A moment away from you is too long."

"What am I to do?" she asked, tears filling her blue eyes to overflowing.

He whispered his answer onto her lips. "Wait for me."

****

Jane tugged the buckle on Braden's saddle tighter and then patted the large stallion's neck. "Carry him, well," she said. "And bring him back to me soon." A clamor behind her made her turn. Braeden had come for his horse. "You're ready to leave?" she asked him.

He walked to the stall and she handed him the reigns. "The battle for Joyous Guard begins soon and Constantine and I must join our brother knights quickly if we are to be of any help to our King." He pushed open the stall door then stood back with one hand splayed on the door, the other on the hilt of his sword.

Jane swallowed hard as she walked past him. So close to him that she could hear him breathing, feel the warm of his breath fall against her skin. She fought the urge to stop and inhale his essence; the raw, pleasant untamed scent of leather and spice. Never in her life did she ever feel this way; breathless, alive and alert.

The image of Braeden in battle came into her mind. He was like a lion in the fight. Deadly and disconcerting, wild and unpredictable. Their joining had been the same, yet the tenderness she felt in the aftermath unlike any she had known. She couldn't catch her breath as emotions ripped though her. How could she let him leave her?

She turned suddenly, blocking his way. "Braeden, will you come back?"

He pulled her to him and rested his cheek lightly against her head. "Do you wish that?"

"I do, but there are things you need to know about me. My mother, my family..."

Braeden released her and cupped her face with his hands, silencing her with a kiss. "I know all I need to know. You are my match. My equal in every way. No other woman ever touched me the way you have, and I expect no one ever will."

Jane looked into his eyes and saw a fire burn that nearly scorched her. "We do not know what tomorrow might bring, but at least we have now." She rose up and kissed him with all the fierce longing that had been building inside her. No gentle, savoring kiss would do on the day of their parting. She kissed him with pure passion that took her breath away.

With a groan he pulled back from her, then scooped her up into his arms and headed for the soft mound of hay at the back of the barn.

"Where are you taking me?" she whispered against his neck.

"Where we can be alone, and as many times as it suits me," he said just before his mouth took hers in a fire that consumed her right down to her toes.

Chapter Twenty-Five

A few months later

Cynthia sat on a bench in her bedchamber combing her long blond hair. The battle of Joyous Guard had been long and bloody and weeks stretched empty since heralds had come with any news. She did know that King Arthur and Lancelot both lost their lives along with many knights on both sides, and that a new king had been crowned on the battlefield. She begged for news of her beloved Constantine and of Braeden, but any messengers who did come to the shire had none to give.

She set the brush down on the tabletop and placed a hand on her growing belly. Would her child know his father? She raised her eyes and prayed that he would.

A clamor from the quad outside her window seemed to coincide with Jane's voice calling her name.

"Cynthia," Jane cried, her voice trembling as she entered. "The Kings comes to Leyborne Castle. Perhaps he brings news of Constantine and Braeden."

Cynthia ran to the window. A procession of flag bearers had already entered the courtyard, their banners flying the crimson dragon and cross of the Knights of the Round Table. Behind them came foot soldiers and pages. She could hear the horses of the knights in the distance, but could see none as yet.

She scooped up her cloak, her hands shaking as she fastened the clasp at her neck. “Jane, I fear the news is bad. Why else would the newly crowned king come to Leyborne but to tell us of death?” She caressed the curve of her abdomen. “It pains me to think this child might never see his father’s smile.”

“But he will know his father. We will be sure of that.” Jane put her arm around Cynthia’s shoulder. “Come. We will welcome the King together and accept what news he gives us with courage.”

They reached the courtyard in time to see the Knights ride two by two through the gate. Some they recognized as those who had helped defeat Simon and his men, but Constantine and Braeden were not among the first to enter. Cynthia closed her eyes and inhaled deeply, if they were alive, she felt certain they would ride in the lead. Each passing moment they did not appear weighed more heavily on her heart.

Suddenly, she felt Jane release her shoulders. A single word told her why.

“Braeden.” The name fell from Jane’s lips like a prayer.

Cynthia opened her eyes in time to see Braeden jump from a horse escorting the king’s carriage and run to Jane. He swept her into his arms and kissed her. Even from a distance Cynthia could see the love in his eyes.

When their kisses at last satisfied at least a part of their hunger for each other, arm in arm they approached. Cynthia could see a new scar from the battle mark Braeden’s neck and she smiled when she saw that his handsome face had not been touched.

He kissed her on the cheek before speaking. “Milady. You look…” His gaze centered on her belly. “A child?”

She smiled. “Yes,” she said framing her stomach with her hands. “And a very active one.”

“My brother, he is…” Braden began but stopped as the blare of the King’s trumpeters filled the air.

In front of them, the royal carriage rolled to a stop. Braeden nodded in respectful acknowledgment while Cynthia and Jane lowered their head and eyes to show consideration for the newly crowned king.

From her position of respect Cynthia saw black boots emerge from the carriage and followed the gait as the new King walked toward her. “Your majesty, welcome to Leyborne Castle. To what do we owe the honor of this visit,” she asked, forcing her voice to be calm while inside she was crumbling.

“To keep a promise I made to the lady I love,” came the answer.

Cynthia felt her mouth fall open, but no words escaped. She dared not raise her eyes for fear it was all a dream. Could she be mistaken? Could it be Constantine who stood before her?

“Cynthia, look at me,” his familiar voice directed.

She felt him put his hands on her shoulders. When he did, she slowly straightened. As her eyes locked with his, she felt her knees buckle. “Constantine,” she whispered as he caught her in his arms.

He carried her inside the castle and gently placed her on a chair in the anteroom. Braeden and Jane followed closely.

"You are the king," she asked in disbelief.

"Aye. It was the will of Arthur to pass the crown before his death at Joyous Guard," Constantine replied, raining kisses across her face. "Only God will know why he passed rule to me, but I swore to him that I would carry on the code of honor begun at Camelot. We only returned to court a fortnight ago, as it was also his wish for his pyre to be in his homeland near Avalon. I came here as soon as I could." His gaze fell to Cynthia's belly. "A child?"

"Our child."

Constantine's smile grew. "A prince of Camelot."

Cynthia suddenly gasped.

"Is something wrong," Constantine asked, concern lacing his voice. "I can summon the physician."

"No," she assured. "I need no one but Jane to tend to us." A quick intake of breath came again.

"You're not ill?"

"No, 'tis just the quickening. Our baby stirs." She took Constantine's hand and placed it on her stomach. "Greet your child, King Constantine. I have told him much about you."

A word about the author...

Kathye also writes contemporary and career romances for Avalon Books, romantic comedy for Wings Press and fantasy Romances as P. K. Eden for Cerridwen Press with fellow multipublished author Patt Mihailoff, and now Medieval Historical Romance for the Wild Rose Press. She has been a member of New Jersey Romance Writers and Romance Writers of America since 1988 and considers it an honor to have been NJRW President in 1992 and 2001. She credits NJRW and some of its members for helping her Put Her Heart In A Book.

While writing romances has been her dream for many years, the book of Kathye's heart, she is also writing a non-fiction work entitled, Hi Mom, How Are Things in Heaven, a book that developed after the death of her mother and deals with coping with grief though humor.

In her "other" life, Kathye works for Somerset County government and is a member of local city council. She is married to her real-life hero and has three sons.

Visit Kathye at www.kathyequick.com